The Immigrants' Chronicles

FROM THE NETHERLANDS TO AMERICA

THE JOURNEY OF

Pieter & Anna

HELEN DENBOER

Chariot Victor Publishing
A Division of Cook Communications

Be sure to read all the books in
The Immigrants' Chronicles

The Journey of Emilie
The Journey of Hannah
The Journey of Pieter and Anna

Chariot Victor Publishing
A division of Cook Communications, Colorado Springs, Colorado 80918
Cook Communications, Paris, Ontario
Kingsway Communications, Eastbourne, England

THE JOURNEY OF PIETER AND ANNA
© 1999 by Helen DenBoer

Edited by Kathy Davis
Cover design by PAZ Design Group
Art direction by Andrea Boven
Cover illustration by Cheri Bladholm

First printing, 1999
Printed in the United States of America
03 02 01 00 99   5 4 3 2

Library of Congress Cataloging-in-Publication Data

DenBoer, Helen.
    The journey of Pieter & Anna / Helen DenBoer.
    p. cm. —   (The immigrants chronicles)
  "From the Netherlands to America."
    SUMMARY: After his family emigrates from Holland, Pieter con-
vinces them to help a girl they met on a canal boat who is trying to
get to Michigan to find her father.
    ISBN 0-7814-3083-6
    I. Title. II. Title: Journey of Pieter and Anna. III. Series.
PZ7.D41236 Jo 1999
[Fic] — ddc21

                                                                98-35694
                                                                    CIP
                                                                    AC

DEDICATION

In memory of my mother and father, my grandparents who
still spoke a little Dutch, and all my brave ancestors who
crossed the ocean from the faraway little province of
Zeeland in the Netherlands.

In this book you'll find two Dutch words
you may not know:

Mijnheer   Mister
dominie   a minister

Chapter One

Pieter Dekker pushed his empty soup bowl away and swallowed hard. America. Pa said they were moving to America.

Pieter tried to ignore the pounding in his head. "I don't want to move, Pa," he said. He knew he shouldn't interrupt. His sister Elizabeth jabbed him with her elbow. Ma's ladle stopped in midair. Thick pea soup dribbled onto the lace tablecloth. Pa put down the letter he had been reading aloud.

"No one asked for your opinion, Pieter," he said.

Pieter sighed. Pa never wanted to listen to him. He glared at the letter, not daring to look at Pa. "From the State of Michigan," his brother Willem had written neatly at the top. Then, directly underneath, "January 1848."

Michigan. What kind of place had such a strange name? Dark and full of trees, Willem wrote. His brother had been there since last summer, and now Pa said they were all going.

Beneath the table his dog Sep thumped his broad tail and whined softly. Pieter reached down and patted the large silky head, avoiding Pa's eyes.

"But I don't want to leave Zeeland," he argued. "What about school, and my drawing lessons? What about Dirk? He's my best friend. I'll never see him again."

He bit his lower lip to stop it from trembling and bent to kiss Sep's nose. How could he ever become a famous artist so far away from everything? Would there be a school? A church? Places where he and Sep could run?

"Sep won't like America, either," he blurted.

Silence settled over the room. Hearing his name, Sep got up and laid his chin on Pieter's knee. Pieter stroked the soft brown ears. His stomach flip-flopped. What was wrong?

"Sep won't be going to America," Pa said. "It will take months to get to Michigan and he'd have to stay in a crate. It would be cruel. You'll have to find a home for him here, Pieter."

Pieter's chair hit the floor with a thud as he jumped up.

"We can't leave Sep. We can't." Tears filled his eyes. "I won't go. You can all go without me. I'll—I'll go live with Grandpa and Grandma in Goes. I won't go to America. I won't!"

"Pieter!" Pa said, his voice like ice. "Sit down! Now!"

Pieter picked up his chair and sat down. He didn't dare disobey. He buried his face in Sep's soft fur, trying to control his tears.

"Don't be such a baby." His brother Neil kicked him under the table. "This is the most exciting thing that ever happened to us."

"I'm not a baby. I'll be twelve next fall." Pieter rubbed his sleeve across his eyes and scowled at his brother. He knew Neil thought it was time for him to stop going to school and help on the farm. Neil didn't like school and had quit a long time ago. Thirteen-year-old Elizabeth had left two years ago. But Ma had talked Pa into letting Pieter continue.

He kicked back at Neil and missed.

Neil laughed. "You still act like a baby. All you do is sit around and read and draw. You don't even help Ma and Elizabeth. Chopping down trees will be good for you. You're too pale and skinny from being inside all the time."

"Stop it, boys." Pa picked up Willem's letter.

Ma refilled Neil's bowl with soup and reached for Pieter's. He shook his head, wishing Ma would say something to help. She knew how much he loved Sep.

Ma's round face was pale, and Pieter saw her knuckles whiten as her hand clenched on the soup ladle. Her brown hair was smoothed neatly under the wings of her white cap. The curly gold ornaments pinned at the sides gleamed in the evening light. She said nothing.

He sniffed and swallowed around the lump in his throat as

Pa went on reading Willem's letter. Pa sat stiff and tall as always, his long face somber. His beard moved up and down as he read.

> "There is a large colony of Hollanders in the area already. I've purchased 80 acres of land southwest of the Holland settlement. It's filled with trees right now, but the soil is good for farming. I worked all winter for an American named Carter to earn a little extra money. Please bring as much money as you can to buy tools and seed. Food and medicine are scarce and many people have been sick and died. We should be all right if you can get here by June. We need to clear the land, build a cabin, and plant crops in order to make it through the winter. It will help that the woods are full of deer, rabbits, and other animals. I've bought a gun."

Crash! Neil's glass toppled as he leaned forward, his sandy hair flopping into his eyes. Elizabeth grabbed a towel to mop up the water.

"I can learn to hunt!" Neil shouted. "You know I can, Pa. I've got the steadiest hand and the best eye of anyone around."

"We'll all have to work hard." Pa tugged on his beard. "It won't be easy for any of us, but at least in America no one will stop us from setting up our own churches."

Pieter pushed bread crumbs to one side of his plate. How could Pa do this to them? He knew Pa and others thought the *Hervormde Kerk*, the Reformed Church, was too modern. Before Pieter was born, they had broken away to return to the old ways.

Over the years people had tried to stop Pa and the others. Some preachers had been jailed and fined. Many Seceders had decided to leave, so last year Willem had gone with a group of other Netherlanders to see what it was like in America. Pieter had been sure his brother would be back soon, and everything would be the same as before.

He traced the outline of the blue willow tree on his plate, trying to keep Neil from seeing the tears that pushed against his eyelids. What would he do in America without Sep?

"I'll make the arrangements tomorrow, and we'll try to leave in three weeks," Pa went on. "Now let's say a prayer for God's guidance and safe travel."

Pieter folded his hands and bowed his head, but he didn't hear a word of the long prayer. *Pa doesn't care how I feel,* he thought. *He doesn't care about school or my art lessons. He doesn't even care that I'll never see Sep again.*

When Pa and Neil left for the barn and Elizabeth went to feed the chickens, he watched Ma clear the table.

"Do we really have to go to America, Ma?" he asked.

Ma turned slowly, picked up the heavy soup tureen and placed it on the sideboard under the window. She brushed her hand across the blue willows on the side before settling in the kitchen rocker.

Pieter sat on the stool next to her and rested his head against her knee.

This was his world. The flat land he could see through the window, Dirk's farm in the distance. The setting sun turning the sky gold. Ma's rocker, the blue tiles lining the fireplace, his drawings, his books.

How could Pa want to leave all this to live in a strange land covered with trees? They were farmers. Pa didn't know anything about cutting down trees and building houses.

"What if we die like those other people Willem wrote about?" he asked. He tried not to be a baby, but his eyes filled with tears.

"Pieter. God will take care of us." Ma pulled his head from her lap and looked directly into his eyes. "Pa's mind is made up. You know people are still angry at us for leaving the state church. Pa is doing what he thinks is best."

Pieter nodded. God had always taken care of them. He believed that. But what about those people in Michigan who had died? Maybe God hadn't wanted them to go there.

It was all so confusing. He didn't really understand why they didn't belong to the same church as Grandma and Grandpa anymore. Pa said it was because Grandpa's church stopped preaching the truth of the Bible and did modern things like singing hymns instead of the psalms. But Pieter knew Grandpa and Grandma still loved God.

"Why did we have to become Seceders, anyway?" he asked. "If we hadn't, we wouldn't have to move now."

Usually Ma ignored his grumbling, but this time she frowned. "I agree with your pa," she said. "We shouldn't be persecuted for our beliefs. When the potato crop failed, no one would give jobs to Willem or your father or other Seceders. Pa had to borrow a lot of money. In America there's work for everyone."

"Can't Grandma and Grandpa help? They have lots of money." Pieter took the handkerchief Ma gave him and blew his nose.

Ma stood up. "My father already loaned us the money for the land Willem bought in Michigan. We're a lot better off than most Seceders." She waved her hand at the garden outside the window. "At least Pa can sell the farm and pay off our debts. We'll even have enough money for a fresh start in America. Besides, don't you want to see Willem again?"

"Yes, but I'd rather have him come home," Pieter said. "Then I wouldn't have to leave Sep. No one else has to give up anything. Neil doesn't care, and Elizabeth's done with school, and you can take your dishes and furniture."

Ma sighed. "That's enough whining, Pieter," she said. "Perhaps Neil is right. Perhaps I've babied you too much. Anyway, we're leaving everything here." Her eyes flooded with tears, and she blinked rapidly.

"Everything?" Pieter asked.

Ma cleared her throat and tucked a wisp of hair beneath

her cap, setting the gold ornaments swinging.

"We'll sell the house, the furniture, the cows and pigs, and my good dishes," she said. "All we're taking are some changes of clothes and our blankets. We'll take the Bible and the Psalter, and our own food and some pots and dishes. Everything else stays here."

"Sep, too?" He choked on the words.

"You know Dirk loves Sep as much as you do," Ma said. "You can leave Sep with him. He'll be happier in a place he knows." She reached out and stroked Pieter's straight, dark hair. "It will be very hard to leave him, but we'll have a good life in Michigan, you'll see."

Pieter stared at the picture of the windmill on the wall behind Ma's shoulder. How could life ever be good again? He would never forgive Pa for this. Never.

Chapter Two

Through the remainder of March, Pieter continued to go to school. Each afternoon he stayed behind to practice his drawing with his teacher, Mijnheer Buteijn. He needed to learn all he could while he had the chance.

Then one Wednesday in the first week of April Pa announced, "We leave Saturday. We'll spend Sunday with Grandma and Grandpa in Goes and go on to Rotterdam the next day. If all goes well, we should get to Michigan in plenty of time to prepare for the winter."

Pieter shivered. *What if we don't get there in time?* he thought. He pictured them huddled under the trees, snow piling up around them, wind howling through the branches overhead.

"Is Rotterdam where we get on the ship?" he asked to distract himself.

"Yes," Pa said. "A *dominie* named Van Wyck has booked passage for a large group of Seceders from all over the Netherlands."

A small beat of excitement trembled in Pieter's chest. It would be fun to be on a ship. He had never been in anything larger than a rowing boat. But when he thought of Sep, he clamped his mind shut on his excitement and kept his face still. He certainly wouldn't let Pa think he might be looking forward to the trip.

That Friday, Pieter's last day of school, Mijnheer Buteijn pointed to the large world map hanging on the schoolroom wall.

"Gather round, everyone," he said. "We'll have a geography lesson."

Pieter pushed in close. His teacher had drawn the map

and painted the oceans a pale blue, the continents green.

"Dirk, show us where the Netherlands is," Mijnheer Buteijn said.

Dirk put his finger on the west coast of the Netherlands. "We're right here, in the province of Zeeland," he said.

"Correct. Pieter, can you show us where you're going?" the teacher asked. Pieter traced the route over the Atlantic Ocean to North America.

"Where's Michigan?" Nellie asked.

"Here, on the east side of this big lake." Mijnheer Buteijn pointed to one of five large lakes in the middle of the continent. Pieter thought the mapmaker must have made a mistake. The lake looked as big as all of Holland.

"Ma says we'll land in a city called New York." Pieter pointed to a tiny speck on the east coast of America. "Willem wrote that it's noisy and dirty and full of thieves and pickpockets."

"Then why are you going?" Hetty asked.

"Because my father says we have to." Pieter put his index finger on the edge of the lake. "Michigan's not a city. It's nothing but trees. There aren't any thieves in the woods, but there might be bears and wildcats."

He glanced anxiously at Mijnheer Buteijn. "How will we get there from New York?" he asked.

"There are railroads. Or perhaps you'll go on the Erie Canal to the lakes," the teacher answered.

There were canals in America? Something tight gave way in Pieter's chest. Water! They would be on water the whole way.

He could watch the pictures the clouds made against the blue sky. There would be rivers and canals, and maybe Pa's farm would be at the edge of that great lake—Lake Michigan. Perhaps America wouldn't be so bad after all.

All day he was the center of an excited group of children. At the end of the school day Hetty brought him a small book. It was handmade and bound with tightly braided red yarn.

"This is to remember us by," she said. Pieter opened the book. On the first page Mijnheer Buteijn had drawn a picture of the school. The next page contained the words "God go with you," circled by tiny sketches of all Pieter's friends. Each student had signed the book. The rest of the pages were blank.

"This goes with it." The teacher handed Pieter a package wrapped in brown paper. Inside were two sticks of drawing charcoal.

"It's for you to draw pictures of all the places you see on your way to America. So you don't forget how to draw," Jacoba said. Everyone looked at the wall covered with pictures Pieter had drawn of his friends.

Will I ever see any of them again? he wondered. His throat tight, he smiled his thanks for the book. They couldn't have given him a better gift. The book was small enough to keep in the deep pocket of his baggy trousers. He would carry it always.

After school, with calls of "God bless you" ringing in his ears, he set out with Dirk toward home. Halfway there Sep met them, barking a greeting and jumping first on Pieter, then on Dirk.

"He doesn't know what's going to happen," Pieter said around the lump in his throat. "Could you leave us alone awhile? I'll catch up in a minute."

As Dirk walked on ahead toward his farm, Pieter slid down a grassy bank and sat under a small tree.

Sep barked at him, asking to play. Pieter threw a stick and watched Sep dash after it and bring it back. Back and forth the big dog ran until he collapsed, panting, at Pieter's feet.

Pieter pulled out the small book his friends had given him. Very carefully he began to draw, the way Mijnheer Buteijn had taught him.

First the familiar lines of Sep's head, the dark intelligent eyes, the mouth that seemed to smile, the ears that twitched in eagerness. Then the large strong body, the flat wide paws, the broad chest, and down to the tail that thumped against the grass.

As he drew, he forgot America. Forgot the darkness that had

hovered over him for the last several weeks. Forgot the hard lump of grief in his chest every time he thought of leaving Sep.

He and Sep were alone under the vast sky with the sun shining and the branches of the tree whispering above him. Alone and suspended in time where nothing ever changed. He shaded in the last dark strokes of Sep's long hair just as a small cloud passed in front of the sun. Sep sat up and barked, eager to be off, and the spell broke.

Pieter rose and pushed the book deep into his pocket. At least now he had a picture of Sep to take with him. He could take it out and look at it whenever things got bad.

He tried to whistle to Sep, but his lips shook, so he pressed them tightly together and headed toward Dirk's farm. Sep ran alongside Pieter, racing ahead as they saw Dirk waiting for them, a piece of rope in his hands.

The boys stood quietly, not knowing what to say to each other, until finally Dirk spoke. "You know I'll take good care of him."

Pieter nodded, not trusting his voice.

"As soon as you get to Michigan, write to me and I'll write back. I'll tell you everything about Sep. How many rabbits he caught, how well he's doing with the cows, everything."

Pieter nodded again. Sep stopped racing around the boys and sat down as if sensing something odd.

Pieter dropped to his knees and threw his arms around the dog, hiding his tears in the softness of Sep's coat. He thought he'd like to throw his arms around Dirk, too, holding on to them both, steadying his world forever. But boys didn't do that.

Sep wriggled out of his grasp and sat back. He stretched out a paw as if asking what was wrong. Pieter reached up, took the rope from Dirk's hand, and tied one end around Sep's neck. He leaned forward one last time and pressed his cheek against the side of Sep's head. The dog licked his neck. Pieter stood up quickly and placed the rope in Dirk's hand.

"It'll be all right," Dirk said, grasping his hand firmly.

"Yes, good-bye." Pieter pushed the words through tight lips. He turned and walked quickly away.

But it was not all right. *I've lost everything,* he thought, *my friends, my teacher, my school, my dog.* At the edge of the field he stopped. He tried not to look back, but he couldn't help himself.

Dirk stood where he had left him, the rope held tightly in his hands. Sep pulled against the rope, his large body straining toward Pieter. His barks echoed sharp and clear across the field, as if he were calling, "Come back. Don't leave me." Pieter turned his back on him and ran.

Chapter Three

The ship dipped suddenly and Pieter's stomach lurched. He rolled over with his face to the side of the berth. The smell of vomit hung in the air and made his head ache. Someone was singing psalms on the other side of the ship.

"Ma," he called. No one answered.

He curled his body into a ball and tried to hold in his stomach the trickle of water Elizabeth had given him. The big ship creaked and groaned about him, its voice blending with the moans of the hundreds of seasick people.

Tiers of wooden bunks lined the walls of the passenger space built between the cargo hold below and the open deck above. Families were crammed into the bunks, three or four to a berth. Most of them were Netherlanders, and Pieter wondered how many others wished they were back home.

Pa and the other men said it was important to live where they could worship according to the old beliefs and doctrines. Back in Goes Grandpa had said that farmers in America were much better off than in Zeeland; that God would bless them in their new life.

Pieter didn't feel blessed. Did God really want them to go to Michigan? What if the storm got worse and the ship sank? He closed his eyes tightly to stop his head from spinning. Was he going to die?

Serve them right if I did, he thought. *I never wanted to come in the first place. I hate this ship. I want my own bed in our farmhouse. I want to see the sky. I want Sep.* Tears mingled with the perspiration on his face.

"How are you feeling, son?" He heard Pa's voice as if from

a great distance. He felt an arm around his shoulders. "Sit up," Pa said. "You've got to get some water in you."

Pieter's lips were dry as crackers. He raised his head to sip from the tin cup Pa held.

"Ma," he croaked.

"Your ma's seasick too," Pa said. "Half the people on the ship are sick." He lowered Pieter gently and pressed a cool wet rag against his mouth. "You'll feel better once the storm is over."

"I want Ma," Pieter said. He rolled over, turning his back on Pa.

The straw mattress rustled as Pa rose. Suddenly Pieter didn't want him to leave. He rubbed the rag across his face and swallowed hard. Pa stood for a moment by the side of the bunk, then moved away. Pieter rolled over.

"Pa," he called. But it was too late. Pa had moved past the row of tables in the middle of the aisle to the family on the other side.

The ship lurched again. He crossed his arms over his stomach and turned back to the wall. He didn't care if Pa hadn't heard him. It was all Pa's fault he was sick and miserable.

For the next three days the ship rolled and pitched. Pieter was vaguely aware of Pa and Elizabeth giving him water, helping him to the slop bucket, and sponging his face. He slept off and on, at night wedged in with Pa and Neil.

Then one morning he woke to find that the ship had settled.

His stomach growled. For the first time in days he wanted something to eat. As he climbed over Neil and slid to the floor, his legs collapsed beneath him. He sat where he fell, waiting for the dizziness to leave, watching the chaos around him.

People moved slowly as if waking from a long sleep. Many were pale and thin, their hair matted and greasy. For a moment his stomach turned queasy from the odor of unwashed bodies. Then he smelled porridge.

"Ma," he called, seeing his mother bent over a pot. "I can't walk."

"Yes, you can." Elizabeth appeared with a pile of clean clothes. "Ma's much too weak to help you."

Pieter's cheeks burned as he realized that she was right. Ma sat on a low stool. Her face was gray, small wrinkles showing next to her lips. He forced himself to stand.

"You and Ma were among the sickest," Elizabeth said. She put her hand under his elbow. "You're skinnier than ever."

"Several people died—one woman just this morning," she added as they crossed the tilting deck toward Ma. "They had to bury them at sea. Thank God the rest of us are so healthy."

She lowered Pieter to the floor next to Ma. Pieter found he had lost his appetite again. People had been left behind in this cold sea? Was it anyone he knew?

"Pa made us some porridge," Ma said. "The ship's cook lit the stove again." She reached down and gave him a hug.

Pieter pulled back in shock. A brownish-green stain covered Ma's usually spotless apron and a sour smell rose from her dress. Her dingy gray cap clung to dull, tangled hair. Her hand shook as she stirred the porridge.

What's happening to us? he thought. *Ma should be home in her own kitchen making pancakes instead of sitting in the middle of this stinking ship.* Ma had been brought up surrounded by beautiful things. With gifts from her parents she had made their farmhouse warm with color and beauty. Now everything was gone.

Once again anger at Pa for taking them away from home rose in Pieter's chest. It gave strength to his legs. He stood up and took the spoon from Ma's hand.

"I'll dish out the food," he said. "You sit and rest."

Pa brought a jug of water over and set it on the floor.

"After we eat we'll try to clean up a bit," he said, looking intently at Pieter. He rested his hand on Ma's shoulder and watched him scoop porridge into the dishes.

"Glad to see you're up—and helping." Pa's voice held a hint of surprise.

Pieter lifted his chin. "Ma's very weak," he said, his voice stern. "We'll all have to help her."

"You're right, Pieter," Pa said. His eyes crinkled suddenly at the edges and his tight mouth loosened in a small smile.

Ma reached out and ruffled Pieter's hair. "You sound just like your pa," she said.

Elizabeth burst into laughter. Pieter spun around to tell her to be quiet and found himself laughing instead.

Neil, stretching and yawning, joined the group, his sandy hair standing in spikes from sleep.

"What's so funny?" he asked.

"You are," Pieter said with a giggle.

Then they were all laughing, even Pa. *Laughing because the storm is over,* Pieter thought. *Laughing because we're all together, even though we're dirty and we smell. Laughing because up above the sun must be shining, even though we can't see it.* He laughed so hard he had to sit down.

Pa sobered first. "Let's ask God's blessing on this food and the remainder of the trip," he said. "The storm set us back several days. Things will have to go smoothly if we're to get to Michigan in time." He held out his hand to Ma.

As they joined hands, Pieter sobered too. Would they be able to find Willem once they got there? They hadn't received any letters from him since the January one, although Pieter knew Pa had expected one. Why hadn't he written again? And what would they do if they got there too late to get a cabin up before winter? He shuddered to think what Michigan would be like without a house or food.

He bowed his head and added a silent prayer to Pa's.

Chapter Four

Later that morning, his stomach filled with warm porridge, Pieter sat with Elizabeth, looking at the pictures in the big family Bible. Their filthy clothes were packed away. Ma sat on her stool talking with the other women, her knitting needles clicking through her fingers.

Neil had disappeared with a group of older boys. Pieter supposed they had sneaked on deck, even though the crew kept complaining that the passengers got in the way. The beds had been tidied, and someone had opened the hatch. A damp, salty breeze blew through the hold, dispersing some of the smells.

Pa had put on his Sunday coat even though it was a Thursday. He held his soft black hat in his hand. For the last half hour he had huddled with a group of men at one end of the long tables that ran down the middle of the room. Now he leaned over Pieter and Elizabeth.

"I'm going to need the Bible for awhile," he said. "And I want Pieter to come with me."

Pieter followed Pa across the hold, his mouth dry. Pa's face was set in its familiar stern lines, his laughter forgotten. All about him Pieter saw that other men had put on their black coats and carried their Bibles.

"We're going on deck," Pa said. He stopped at the bottom of a ladder. "The captain gave us special permission. Go on." He boosted Pieter up the ladder. "You need some fresh air. They won't give us many chances to be up here."

Pieter scrambled up and lifted his face to the light that shone through the open hatch. After the dimness of the space beneath the deck, the brightness blinded him.

Pa followed him up the ladder and steadied him as the ship rocked. He led Pieter to the side of a rectangular structure like a little house that was built on top of the open deck. Two lifeboats rested on its roof.

"I want you to stay right here by the deckhouse. You're not to go anywhere else," Pa said. "I've got business to attend to." He rounded a corner of the deckhouse and disappeared.

Pieter drew in deep breaths of fresh air and gazed in awe at the stretch of gray sea on all sides. Small waves, left over from the storm, rose and broke on its surface. He scrunched himself farther into a coil of ropes. Above his head, three tall masts soared into the sky, their huge canvas sails snapping in the breeze. Low gray clouds moved swiftly eastward, revealing patches of blue sky to the west.

The sound of footsteps brought his attention back to the deck. He watched as one after another of the black-coated men passed in front of him. They headed toward the back of the ship, carrying their Bibles and Psalters. One or two women, their eyes down, clung to their husbands' arms.

What was going on? Maybe the quiet that had settled over the hold after breakfast had been more than just because everyone was tired. Something was happening at the back of the ship. Something most of the women and children were not involved in. Something that could only be talked about in whispers.

Pieter crept quietly toward the back of the deckhouse. At the far end of the ship, a group of people stood with bowed heads. Dominie Van Wyck stood in the center, his head bent over a Bible, reading aloud. In front of him a long bundle, draped in black, lay on the deck.

A cold shiver of fear snaked down Pieter's spine. Hadn't Elizabeth said something about a woman dying during the storm? Was that her body wrapped in the bundle?

He couldn't take his eyes off the terrible sight. After awhile, the dominie closed the Bible and folded his hands. The men took off their hats. They prayed so long Pieter's legs stiffened.

Finally, the minister raised his head and six men came forward. Slowly they lifted the bundle and brought it to the top of the railing. As Pieter watched in horror, they slid the bundle into the sea. His heart pounded and cold perspiration covered his body. This was what Elizabeth had meant by people being buried at sea.

As the group began singing the words of Psalm 100, Pieter heard someone sobbing. His legs shaking, he tiptoed across the deck toward the sound.

A girl crouched behind a pile of sailcloth, watching the funeral just as he was. She was smaller than Pieter, and thinner, with wispy blond hair straggling from beneath her cap. She held her hands tightly over her lips, trying to muffle her sobs. Her body shook.

Pieter moved forward and put his hand on the girl's shoulder. "What's wrong?" he asked. "Can I help?"

The girl whirled around and shoved at Pieter in panic. He lost his balance and landed hard on his bottom.

The girl stood over him. Her pale skin was red and blotchy from crying. "Leave me alone," she said. "She's gone and there's nothing anyone can do." She drew in a deep shuddering breath. "Just leave me alone," she said as she stepped over Pieter and disappeared through the hatch.

Pieter crawled back to his place at the side of the deckhouse. Despite the sun that was beginning to break through the clouds, he still shivered. Was the dead person the girl's mother? He knew how he would feel if his mother died. What would happen to her now?

When Pa returned, Pieter kept silent until they were back below deck. He couldn't see the girl anywhere, but that wasn't unusual. There were more than 400 passengers between decks. She could be anywhere. He found Ma darning a hole in a pair of trousers.

"Ma," he whispered, sitting close to her so no one else would hear. "There was a girl up on deck crying. Was it her ma who died?"

Ma stroked Pieter's dark hair. "Your Pa shouldn't have taken you up there," she said. "But I suppose I can't protect you forever." Her brown eyes were sad.

"Was it her mother?" Pieter asked again.

"Yes," Ma said. "She had bad lungs and a terrible cough before she came aboard. She should never have come on this trip. I heard that the girl is all alone now. I don't know where the father is."

"What will happen to her?" Pieter reached out and took Ma's hand.

"I don't know. I think they'll have to send her back. Perhaps when we get to New York there will be a family going back. The dominie and the elders will find a way. She'll be cared for. Don't worry about her."

But he couldn't forget. Occasionally he caught glimpses of the girl's pale face. He never saw her cry again. Instead, her face was set in tight, determined lines.

Whenever he saw her, he remembered the hard knot that had stayed in his chest for so long whenever he thought about losing Sep. How much worse it would be to leave your mother in that cold gray sea. Sep was still alive. Dirk would write and tell Pieter about him. But this girl would never see her mother again.

He pulled his book out of his pocket and paged through it looking at the pictures he had drawn of Sep. He smiled thinking of him running beside Dirk, snapping at the cows' heels, barking at the chickens. When he got to a blank page, he took his pencil and drew the silent group of people around the black bundle on deck.

This time the ache in his heart was for the girl, not Sep.

Chapter Five

For days after the funeral Pieter saw almost nothing but the cramped area between the deck and the hold. Occasionally, the passengers were allowed on deck for some fresh air. He spent most of his time drawing pictures of the people. He looked for the girl who had lost her mother, but seldom saw her. He tried to draw her face but couldn't get it right.

One day he told Elizabeth what had happened and showed her the picture he had drawn, but Elizabeth couldn't find her either.

Finally, there came a day when Neil and the other boys thundered down the ladder, shouting that the coast of North America had been sighted. Pieter jumped up with a yell, shoved his book and pencils back into his pocket, and joined the men, women, and children pushing their way up the ladder to the deck.

It was true. Off in the distance, he could see a soft black line against the horizon. America! Finally! In a few days they would be off this rolling ship and back on solid ground. But the ground would not be Zeeland. Despite his happiness, a small knot of fear formed in his stomach. America. What would it be like? Would he like it?

Two days later, he was sure he did not like it. At least he didn't like New York. The family stood on a wooden walkway surrounded by bundles and trunks. Pieter pressed close to Elizabeth as people swarmed around them. Ma sat on one of the trunks, her hands clasped tightly in her lap, her face pale.

The noise hurt Pieter's ears. Men shouted in a dozen languages, babies screamed, horses neighed, wagons creaked and rumbled. Overhead, gulls screeched as they swooped toward the water.

The smell of dead fish wafted up from the harbor. Dozens of tall ships rested side by side, their masts sending long shadows across the wharf. Men pushed carts loaded with boxes, or carried barrels on their shoulders. Cats darted out from the shelter of buildings to snatch at bits of fish, then disappeared again.

"I can't see Pa anymore," Pieter said, standing on tiptoe.

He shifted the basket with Ma's dishes in it to his other hand. The basket was heavy, but Pieter knew how important it was to keep a good grip on it. It held the sugar sifter made of silver that Grandma had given Ma back in Goes. Grandma's father had brought it home from far overseas when he had been a merchant. It was old and rare.

"If you have to live in a house made of logs, at least you can have one nice piece of tableware like decent folks," Grandma had said, scowling at Pa.

Pa had accepted the gift with a nod of thanks and entrusted Pieter with the basket. Pieter had been surprised, but he took special care of it. Every day he had checked its hiding place on the ship to make sure it was safe.

Now he set the basket down carefully, holding it firmly between his feet. He rubbed his tired arm. Pa had disappeared into the crowd searching for someone to tell them what to do next. Pa had looked uneasy. *Almost fearful,* Pieter thought. None of them had learned much English on board the ship. Most of the passengers had been Hollanders and spoke the same language they did.

Many of these friends would no longer be with them. Some were met by relatives. Others were staying in New York or taking the train southwest to the prairies. Others stood around like lost sheep. *Pa doesn't know what to do,* Pieter realized with shock.

A two-wheeled cart piled high with barrels rattled past. Dust rose from its wheels. Pieter sneezed. The dirt and noise of the city made his head spin. At least in Rotterdam people dressed alike and spoke the same language.

A stocky man smelling of onions lurched against him. Pieter stumbled sideways, then righted himself against Elizabeth and reached for the basket. It was gone. The silver was gone!

"Neil! Pa!" Pieter shouted. Without thinking, he plunged into the crowd after the man who had bumped into him. He could see the basket swinging from his hand. The man seemed in no hurry, walking quickly toward a busy street. In a minute, he'd be lost in the crowd.

"Stop, thief," he yelled. He squeezed between two women and stumbled over a dog, making it yelp and snap at his heels. The man was still in sight. Pieter could hear the clump of wooden shoes behind as Neil caught up with him.

He shouted again, and up ahead a man in the crowd stepped away from the side of a warehouse. He seemed to understand the situation immediately. As the thief hurried past, the second man grabbed his arm, swung him around, and pinned him against the brick wall of the building.

Gasping for air, Pieter rushed up, followed by Neil, who was still shouting. Then Pa was there, too, and everyone was talking at once. The thief leaned against the building, still pinned by the rescuer. Pieter saw a smirk on his face and wondered how he dared to laugh.

"He stole our basket," Pieter said. He pointed to the basket still clutched in the thief's right hand.

Pa reached out and snatched the basket. The thief shrugged, and the man holding him turned to Pa.

"New York is full of thieves," he said in the language of Holland. Pieter breathed a sigh of relief. "My name is Mijnheer Van Hout. I'm glad I was here to help." He shouted to a man in a blue cap standing on the corner.

"A policeman," he said to Pa. "He'll take this fellow to jail." Pa nodded as the tall thin policeman secured the thief's hands behind his back.

Pa and Neil bent over the basket to check its contents. Pieter looked up to thank his rescuer and froze. All three men were grinning at each other and Pieter's heart skipped a beat.

Something was wrong. He was sure he saw the thief wink at Mijnheer Van Hout just before the policeman led him away. Pieter watched them go, his thoughts in a muddle. Was that really a policeman? The man had a blue cap and a nightstick, but no uniform. He wondered what a policeman in New York was supposed to look like.

"Pa." Pieter yanked on Pa's sleeve. "Something strange is going on."

"Not strange, silly," said Neil. "If you'd taken better care of Ma's things, this wouldn't have happened."

"Hush," Pa said. "None of us expected to be robbed. The thief picked Pieter because he's small." He stood frowning down at Pieter, then held out the basket.

"Take it, son," he said in a gruff voice. "You were very brave to chase that man." He turned back to Mijnheer Van Hout.

"But, Pa—" Pieter argued, then stopped. Pa was trusting him again. He'd look like a fool telling everyone Mijnheer Van Hout was involved in some kind of plot against them.

He tightened his grip on the basket and turned away. He must have imagined the smirk and winks. After all, Mijnheer Van Hout had rescued them. How could he possibly be friends with a thief? He tried to quiet the voice in his head that said something was wrong and followed Pa and Mijnheer Van Hout back to the wharf.

Chapter Six

As they made their way back toward Ma and Elizabeth, Pieter could hear Pa and Mijnheer Van Hout making plans.

Ma stood, her hand on her heart, and reached quickly to pull Pieter toward her. Elizabeth jumped up and down and clapped her hands in excitement. Neil rattled on as if he had caught the thief himself. Pieter stood and watched Mijnheer Van Hout.

"What's wrong?" Elizabeth asked. "It's not your fault the basket was stolen. The thief could have grabbed it from Neil, too. Or me."

"It's not that," Pieter said, although he was sure it was only because he was sickly looking that the thief had chosen him. Then another thought occurred.

Why had the thief stolen the basket? He couldn't have known Grandma's sugar sifter was in it. It might have held nothing more valuable than bread and cheese. There was something going on as nasty as the fish smell that wafted up to them from the filthy water below the wharf. But what?

Pa and Mijnheer Van Hout seemed to be deep in a serious discussion. When Pieter saw Pa pull out his money pouch and take out some gold coins, he shoved the basket into Elizabeth's hands.

"Hold this," he said. "I've got to talk to Pa."

"No!" Elizabeth tried to grab his jacket. "You know you're not supposed to interrupt grown-ups when they're talking."

Pieter slipped away and went to stand next to Pa. He cleared his throat loudly.

"Pa, I have to talk to you," he said. "Alone." His voice shook at the look in Pa's eyes.

"This is men's business, Pieter," Pa said. "And not to be interrupted. Where is the basket?"

"Elizabeth has it. Please, Pa. It's important." He glanced at Mijnheer Van Hout and shivered at the cold blue eyes that met his.

"Go back to your mother, Pieter." Pa's voice was firm.

Pieter's eyes filled with tears and he whirled away. *He's still treating me like a baby*, he thought. *Then let him. Mijnheer Van Hout is not the friend Pa thinks he is. I'm sure of it. There's something crooked about him.*

He took the basket back from Elizabeth and sat on the edge of a trunk. He clamped his lips together. Pa would be sorry he hadn't listened to him. Choking back his anger, he watched Pa count out guilders for Mijnheer Van Hout. The two men shook hands and Pa returned, waving a handful of paper in the air. He was followed by a boy pulling a two-wheeled cart.

"Tickets all the way to Michigan," Pa said. "They cost more than I thought, but Mijnheer Van Hout assured me it was the best price I could get." He tucked the tickets into the inside pocket of his jacket. "We were fortunate to meet a Hollander so quickly. Who knows how long it would have taken to find our way otherwise. Load the luggage on the cart. We leave for Albany in a few hours." Pa looked happy and excited, in charge again.

"Do we get to go on a steamer this time, Pa?" Neil asked.

"From here to Albany," Pa answered. "We'll stay in an inn there overnight and take a canalboat on the Erie Canal to Buffalo. From there, we'll catch another steamer across the Great Lakes to Michigan."

Pa smiled at Ma and Pieter and hoisted a trunk onto the cart.

"No waves on the Hudson River or Erie Canal," he said. "No seasickness. Just quiet water and lots of sunshine. You two will be healthy again in no time. Follow me."

They pushed and shoved their way through the crowded streets until they reached the river on the west side of the city. Pieter was sure the boy with the cart would slip away somehow with all their belongings, but nothing happened. The boy led them to a small steamer in the river harbor and helped them load their luggage onto the deck.

Pieter recognized a few other families from the ship as they came on board. Everyone was in a festive mood. The sun shone, the sky arched blue above them. The Hudson River stretched before them, its waters calm and broad.

Once Ma was settled below deck drinking coffee with two other women, Pieter raced with Elizabeth up the ladder to watch as the steamboat pulled away from the pier. The river harbor was thronged with boats, from tall sailing vessels to tiny crafts propelled by only one man.

"Someday I'll have a boat of my own," he told Elizabeth. "I'll live beside the water and paint pictures of Lake Michigan. I don't want to hunt like Neil or build things like Willem. I'm going to be an artist." He pushed away his worry about Mijnheer Van Hout and laughed as two boats almost collided, their owners shouting and waving their oars at each other.

"What if we live in the woods?" Elizabeth asked. She leaned over the rail and waved at a small sailboat below.

Pieter pulled her back, and they settled on some boxes, watching the grimy brick warehouses of New York City slip past.

"I know Willem said our property is in the woods," he said, "but my teacher said the Holland Colony is on a lake called Black Lake. And it's close to Lake Michigan. I think Willem bought land on the lake." His earlier fears of disaster began to fade. "When I'm not at school or drawing, I'll build my boat." He sat up as he recognized a familiar face.

"Look," he said, grabbing Elizabeth's arm. "There's that girl."

"What girl?" Elizabeth stretched her legs out and settled her back more firmly against a large trunk.

"The one whose mother died on the ship. She must have found a family to take her in." He watched as the girl followed a fat woman and three small children to the other side of the boat.

"Poor girl," Elizabeth said. "I wonder where they're going?

Maybe she has relatives in Albany who will take her in." She pulled her embroidery out of her pocket and threaded a needle with yellow floss.

The boats in the harbor grew smaller as the steamer moved away from New York City. Pieter yawned. The sun shone. The river flowed smoothly. He closed his eyes and dozed, dreaming of quiet waters, a small boat, a net full of fish.

"Pieter." Elizabeth was shaking him. "You've been sleeping for an hour. Come on. Let's see what the others are doing."

Pieter stretched and stood up, eager to see what lay ahead. He spun around to follow Elizabeth and froze. His chest tightened and his knees went weak as he stared at the scene in front of him.

Chapter Seven

Trees. Everywhere. Dark and menacing. Up ahead, to his left and to his right, as far as Pieter could see, nothing but trees.

They hung from the banks along the river's edge as if reaching to snatch him from the boat. They climbed the steep hills that rose on both sides of the water. To the west, he could see more hills, higher and darker, and still tree-covered. The tallest ones looked black as they faded into the mist, far away in the distance.

In all his worst nightmares, Pieter had never imagined that America would be this big, that hills could be this high.

"What's wrong?" Elizabeth asked.

Pieter took a deep breath. He could never explain how he felt. The trees seemed to laugh at him, threatening to topple over onto the deck, pulling the hills with them. Their shadows moved on the brown water below, like huge sea monsters gliding alongside the boat.

He focused on Elizabeth's face. "Nothing's wrong," he said. "Let's go below." He led the way below deck not looking at all those trees again.

For the rest of the trip to Albany, Pieter stayed below as much as possible. When he did go on deck, he kept his eyes on the water, watching the way it changed colors as the sun slid in and out of the clouds. First a muddy brown, then gray, then a bright silver that broke into sparkles as the breeze ruffled the water. But he knew the trees were always there. If he looked toward the shore, he saw their reflection turn the water green.

Once in sight of Albany, he breathed easier. The river here

was broad. Warehouses and docks hugged the shoreline. Openings had been cut in the tree-covered hillside for streets and houses. Far ahead to the right he could still see mountains, but on their left a cluster of brick houses climbed a steep hillside.

"It's beautiful," Elizabeth said.

They followed Pa off the boat and up the hill to an inn Pa had heard about back in Zeeland. "Friends of friends," Pa said. Pieter hoped they wouldn't be friends as odd as Mijnheer Van Hout back in New York City. He panted as he dragged the basket of dishes up the steep incline.

Pieter liked Albany. The houses looked like the ones in Goes where Grandma and Grandpa lived. The family that greeted them at the inn still spoke the language of Holland, although they'd been in America for a long time. The tall wardrobes in the bedrooms and the long sideboard in the dining room reminded him of home.

After supper Neil and Elizabeth found an old checkerboard on a table and set up a game. Ma chatted quietly with the innkeeper's wife. Pieter settled on a low bench near the gigantic fireplace and pulled out his drawing book and pencils. He hadn't wanted to draw the menacing hills with their towering trees, but now he drew his family. It was almost like being back in Zeeland.

The fire sputtered, the checkers clacked on the board. Pieter drew until he became aware of Pa's voice, talking to the innkeeper, Mijnheer Geerlings.

"That's not possible," Pa was saying. His voice held a hint of panic. "I paid for tickets all the way to Michigan. I gave him all our travel money."

Pieter looked across to where Pa sat at the table. He had the papers that Mijnheer Van Hout had sold him in New York City spread across the table. His face was ashen.

The innkeeper shook his head. "You've been swindled," he said. "I'm truly sorry. It happens all the time. These papers are no good. The only tickets that were any good were the ones for the steamer here to Albany. This man you met in New York wanted you far away before you discovered he was a thief."

Pieter sat very still, not moving a muscle. He had been right all along about Mijnheer Van Hout.

"But he was so helpful," Pa insisted. His hands began to tremble. "He was a Hollander." He explained about the stolen basket.

"It sounds like a trick to me," Mijnheer Geerlings said. "The swindlers have all kinds of schemes to rob people just off the ships. I'm sure they were all in on it. The robber, the policeman, and Mijnheer Van Hout. They most likely didn't even know you had any silver in the basket. They just grabbed whatever was easiest. Then Mijnheer Van Hout pretends to help and sells you the fake tickets."

Pieter wanted to jump up and remind Pa that he had tried to warn him. But the crumpled look on Pa's face kept him silent. Pa shuffled the papers on the table, first one way, then the other. He ran his hands through his hair. His shoulders sagged.

"It was all the travel money we had," he said in a low voice. Neil and Elizabeth had stopped their game. Ma's needlework lay in her lap, untouched. A shiver traveled up Pieter's spine. What would happen to them now? If they couldn't go on, would they return to Zeeland?

"We still have the money we saved for things we need in Michigan," Ma said in her quiet voice. "We can use that to pay our passage on the Erie Canal and Great Lakes."

"And then what?" Pa sounded defeated. "We can't clear the land without axes. We can't plant crops without seeds. If we don't get a house up and crops in, we'll never make it through the winter."

Fear gripped Pieter's heart at the sight of Pa's face. He forgot about wanting to gloat about being right. Had they given up their house, their farm, for nothing? Had they come all this way to starve?

"There's Willem, Pa," he blurted. "He worked all winter for

that American, Mr. Carter, remember? He'll have his wages. We can buy food and tools with Willem's money." He wasn't sure why he was encouraging Pa. They didn't even know if Willem was still in Michigan. All he knew was that he couldn't stand the look on Pa's face.

Neil's chair scraped on the floorboards as he jumped up, sending checkers flying in all directions. "We can work for more money if we need it, Pa. Willem and I are strong," he said. He glanced at Pieter, as if to say Pieter could work, too, then looked back at Pa. "Willem wrote there's always work for strong men. We'll find a way."

There was no sound in the room except the crackling of the fire. A muscle twitched in Pa's jaw. Then he stood up and gathered all the useless papers together, crumpling them into a ball. He crossed to the fireplace and tossed the ball into it. He straightened his drooping shoulders.

"That's settled, then," he said. "We'll leave for Michigan as soon as possible."

"Hooray!" Neil thumped Pieter on the back. Elizabeth hugged Ma. Pa sat back down, a look of determination once again on his face as he discussed arrangements with the innkeeper.

Pieter breathed a sigh of relief. It was good to see Pa in charge again, but fear tugged at the back of his mind. Once they got to Michigan, the money would be gone. Could they get a house built by winter? What if nothing grew in the woods? They had heard so many stories since leaving the Netherlands about the troubles in the Michigan colony. About sickness and lack of food. About the cold and snow.

Please, God, he prayed. *Help us get to Michigan safely and find a place to live before winter.* He sank onto the hearth and stared into the flames of the fireplace. There was no going back now. Sparks shot upward and disappeared, like his dreams of returning to Zeeland, into the darkness of the chimney.

Chapter Eight

"Bridge up ahead," called the deckhand. "Everybody get down!" Pieter and Elizabeth ignored the steps and jumped from the roof of the canalboat to the deck at the front. There were already three other children there. The adults preferred to stay in the cabin rather than squeeze onto the tiny deck.

"I just saw her again," Pieter said to Elizabeth. "The girl from the ship. She's hiding up on the roof."

He had first noticed her the morning they left Troy on the canalboat bound for Buffalo. She had followed a large family of Hollanders onto the boat, then turned away clutching a bulging green traveler's bag.

Each time Pieter saw the girl she seemed to be hiding. At night, when it got dark and everyone squeezed into the cabin, he could never find her. Most likely she was behind the curtain helping the younger children in the women's quarters.

Now he watched some of the bigger boys, including Neil, hang by their hands over the side of the boat, balancing with their feet on the ridge that circled the cabin above the waterline. Others flattened themselves among the barrels and trunks strapped to the roof of the cabin until they passed beneath the bridge.

The Erie Canal stretched flat and wide between the farms and forests on either side. Overhead the May sun shone warm on their heads. The air smelled of cows. The *clop-clop* of the horses' feet on the towpath sounded like drum beats to Pieter.

Five days earlier they had taken a stagecoach from Albany to Troy where they boarded the canalboat with other immigrants. Crowds of shouting men milled about on the dock, selling tickets. Pieter saw Pa's back-in-charge look on his face again. He already had their tickets and clear instructions from Mijnheer Geerlings about how to get legitimate transport over the Great Lakes once they got to Buffalo.

As the canalboat had moved slowly west, they had passed through a broad valley with the hills far off to their left. Pieter watched in awe as the boat was raised and lowered through the locks alongside the Mohawk River. Numerous small bridges spanned the canal. Some crossed in the middle of a farmer's fields, others in towns and villages.

Once they passed through a small village named Amsterdam. Pieter had hoped to see people dressed in the clothes of Holland, and he called out *"goede morgen"* to them. The people along the canal street waved back, but they were all dressed like Americans, and their greetings were in English.

"They've forgotten their roots," Ma had said, watching the people sadly. "There were a lot of people from the old country that moved here over 200 years ago. I suppose we'll change too." Pieter had noticed that she stood at the rail quietly until the village of Amsterdam was long out of sight.

Now Pieter waved as a boy leaned over the rail of the bridge, laughing at the children below. A dog that looked like Sep propped his feet beside the boy and barked shrilly. As soon as the boat was past the bridge, Pieter climbed back to the roof, looking for the girl.

"Come on," he called to Elizabeth. "I know where she's hiding. Let's go talk to her."

Pieter led the way through the jungle of boxes and barrels until they found the girl. She was sitting with her back against a trunk, her eyes closed.

"That's odd," Pieter whispered to Elizabeth. "She's still carrying her traveling bag."

"Maybe those younger children get into her things if she leaves it below," Elizabeth said.

When they got close, Pieter saw that the wings of the

girl's cap hung limp and her stained dress had a large rip down the side. By this time most of their clothes showed the signs of several weeks of travel, but the girl looked as if no one took care of her. She sat with her knees drawn up tight against her chest. Her hair straggled from beneath her cap in tiny wisps all around her face.

"My name's Pieter Dekker," he said, plopping down beside her. "This is my sister Elizabeth. I saw you weeks ago on the ship, remember?" He didn't dare mention the funeral. He remembered how the girl had angrily pushed him down. Although now she looked as if she couldn't push a baby over.

"What's your name?" Elizabeth asked.

The girl pulled her arms tighter around her knees, making herself smaller.

"Anna De Jong," she said, so quietly that Pieter almost couldn't hear her.

"We're from Zeeland," Elizabeth said. "What province are you from?"

"South Holland," Anna answered.

"Why are you up here alone?" Pieter asked, bursting with curiosity. "Who's that family you're with?" He remembered Ma saying the girl was alone after her mother died. He couldn't imagine how Anna had gotten here without help.

Before Anna could answer, her stomach rumbled, and she bent over as if in pain.

"Are you hungry?" Elizabeth asked, her eyes widening.

"I don't have any food left," Anna whispered.

"But the food's included in the price of the ticket," Pieter said. He knew the food wasn't as good as what Ma had packed in the hamper back in Albany, but there was plenty of it. Anna shouldn't be hungry.

"I know," Anna answered. "But if I go below someone might notice me."

What did she mean? Before Pieter could ask her, Elizabeth jerked her head at him. "Go ask Ma for some sandwiches.

Quick," she said. "And bring something to drink."

Without a word, Pieter jumped up and ran below deck.

Ma was sitting along a bench with some other women, laughing and chatting. Her knitting needles flashed in the sunlight streaming through the window.

"Ma, may we have some bread and cheese?" he asked.

"Please," Ma said automatically, but she opened the large hamper. "It's good to see you so happy and hungry again." She smiled and held out two large cheese sandwiches.

"And a ham one too, please?" Pieter asked, trying to look especially hungry.

"All right, just make sure you share it," Ma said.

"Yes, Ma. Thank you." He grabbed his tin cup and stopped at the water barrel on deck before carefully climbing the stairs back to the girls.

Pieter and Elizabeth shared one of the cheese sandwiches while Anna ate the others. After she had a long drink of the cool water, she stretched her legs out in front of her and leaned back against the green traveling bag. Her head drooped.

"Thank you," she said. She closed her eyes and was soon asleep.

Elizabeth tugged on Pieter's shirtsleeve and pulled him away.

"Let's just watch her for a while," she said. "There's something peculiar going on. Why won't she tell us anything about herself?"

For the rest of that day they crouched behind crates and trunks spying on Anna. She slept most of the afternoon. Then, as some women strolled onto the deck below, talking in shrill voices, she woke suddenly. She scrunched herself as small as possible behind a barrel and rested her head against the green bag.

"She's definitely hiding," Elizabeth whispered. "Why?"

Pieter slid out from behind a crate of squawking chickens. "I don't know, but this is getting boring," he said. "I'm going to ask Ma if I can get off the boat and walk with the teamster for a while. I'll jump back on at the next bridge."

"All right." Elizabeth pulled her embroidery from her pocket. "I'll sit here and see what Anna does," she said. She unrolled the cloth and searched for her needle.

Later, at supper, after his long walk along the towpath and with only half a sandwich at noon, Pieter ate twice as much as he normally did.

"We'll have you strong again in no time," Ma said. Her cheeks were pink again and her hair shone in the lamplight.

Neil laughed. "Pieter will never be strong," he said. He punched Pieter's shoulder and danced away as Pieter swung back.

"Boys." Pa's stern voice stopped them, and Pieter went to sit near Elizabeth.

"Which family is Anna with?" he asked, searching the cabin. There were less than a hundred people on the canal boat and not that many places to hide.

Women were packing away the remains of supper. Men were getting out their pipes to go on deck for a smoke. Mothers were settling the small children and girls behind the curtain at one end of the cabin. Pieter couldn't see Anna anywhere.

"I never saw her come below," Elizabeth answered. "When I left, she was still hiding in a corner between some crates. I've been watching the door all evening. I think she's still on the roof."

"It'll be cold up there." Pieter jumped up. "And she didn't have any supper."

"Elizabeth, it's time for you to go to the women's section." Pa's voice interrupted them. He was helping the other men pull the narrow bunks from inside the storage benches that lined the walls. They hung them one above the other on hooks attached to the insides of the cabin.

Elizabeth hesitated. "I'll check the women's side carefully," she whispered as she followed Ma to the women's quarters. "Meet me early, before breakfast. Just in case she's still up there. We've got to help her."

"It's time for you to settle in too," Pa called to Pieter.

"Yes, Pa." Pieter swallowed hard. He thought of Anna up on

the roof, cold and alone. Did he dare tell Pa about her? With all his other worries about money and why Willem had never written again, would Pa help? Maybe Anna didn't even want their help. He turned away toward his bunk, wondering if she really was still on the roof and if she had a blanket.

Chapter Nine

The next morning only a few people were stirring as Pieter slipped out of his bunk. It was barely daylight, but Elizabeth was already on deck, a shawl pulled tight across her shoulders.

"She's got to be up here. I didn't see her anywhere in the women's quarters last night. She was over on the left side behind the crates," she whispered. "Go quietly; we don't want to scare her." They rounded a large box and found Anna shivering under a thin blanket.

Elizabeth whipped off her shawl and threw it around Anna's shoulders.

"I saved you some bread and butter from supper last night," she said.

Pieter's stomach tightened. He wished he had remembered Anna when he stuffed himself at supper. Elizabeth always thought of others first. He settled himself next to Anna and let Elizabeth take charge.

"Why are you up here by yourself? Where's the family you were with?" Elizabeth asked.

Anna didn't answer. She sat bent over her sandwich, tearing off huge mouthfuls like a starving animal. Her face was thin and pale with tiny freckles spread across her nose. Streaks of dirt covered her cheeks as if she had rubbed tears away all night.

She looked up at them from under thick blond eyelashes, her blue eyes darting from Pieter to Elizabeth before making up her mind to answer. Pieter clamped his lips shut on his impatience.

"I'm on my way to Michigan to join my father," Anna finally said in a low voice.

"That's where we're going," Pieter interrupted. "Is that family you got on with going there too?"

"I'm not with that family," Anna said. "I'm not with anyone." She scrunched up her face as if trying to hold back her tears. "I only followed them on board so people wouldn't notice I was alone. They would have sent me back." She took a deep breath. "My ma's dead," she whispered. "They buried her at sea."

"I remember," Pieter said. He thought of that grim morning on deck—his wobbly legs; Pa's strong arm; the silent group of men gathered around the wrapped bundle on deck; the *dominie's* steady voice reciting, "The Lord is my shepherd, I shall not be in want...." He reached out and patted her hand awkwardly.

Elizabeth handed her a handkerchief and waited until Anna blew her nose.

"How did you get here?" she asked. "Why didn't they send you back to Holland when we reached New York?"

Anna sniffed. "They were going to, but a woman said she'd see to it that I got to Grand Haven. That's where my father lives."

Pieter remembered that Grand Haven was where they would get off the steamer in Michigan before going on to the Holland colony. Maybe Anna could go the rest of the way with them, he thought. Would Pa help? Could they afford to help a stranger?

"That woman in New York lied," Anna continued. "She said she was going to Grand Haven, but she wasn't. When we got to Albany, she said I had to stay with her and help her with her children. So I ran away." She swiped the handkerchief across her eyes. "I have to get to Pa. He's all I have left."

"How old are you?" Elizabeth asked.

"Ten," Anna said.

Younger than I am, Pieter thought, *yet brave enough to run away in a strange country. Her father has to be special to give her that much courage.* He wondered if he would do all the things Anna had done just to get to his own father.

"How'd you get money for the canal boat?" he asked.

"Mama had money in a scarf wrapped around her middle

under her clothes," Anna answered. "Before she died, she gave it to me and made me promise to go find Pa. I bought a ticket in Albany by pretending an adult sent me. I have money for a ticket from Buffalo to Grand Haven, too. I can pay for the food you gave me."

"No," Elizabeth put her hand on Anna's. "We have plenty of food. But we need to tell Ma and Pa. You can't stay on the roof any longer. You'll get sick." She stood up, pulling Anna with her.

"You'll need help in Buffalo getting a ticket for the steamer," she added. "Pa will help you."

Pieter watched as Anna studied Elizabeth's face for a long moment. When she nodded, he picked up the green bag, swung it to his shoulder, and followed the girls below deck.

Pa and Ma were sitting at one of the long tables. "Ma, this is Anna De Jong," Elizabeth said. She pulled Anna forward. Pa looked up from reading his Bible. "Her ma was the one who died on the ship, remember? She's all alone."

"She's trying to get to Michigan," Pieter added. His voice cracked with excitement. "To Grand Haven where her father lives."

Pa closed the Bible with a thump. He looked stunned. "How did you get here, child?" he asked.

Anna burst into tears. Ma reached over and pulled her close. "It's all right, Anna," she said. "You're safe now."

"Tell me what happened," Pa said to Elizabeth and Pieter. He listened patiently as they blurted out Anna's story.

"We have to help her, Pa," Pieter said when they finished. He wiped his sweaty palms on his pants. "We can't leave her to strangers."

"Of course we'll help her," Pa said. "Did you think we wouldn't?" He frowned at Pieter. "Doesn't the Bible teach us to help those in need? We've always taught you that."

"Yes, Pa." Pieter felt ashamed for doubting him. His own feelings of anger toward Pa had made him misjudge him. He knew that all through the troubles in the Netherlands Pa had helped others.

44

Willem had once told him that because Pa and Ma had more money than many others, Pa often paid fines for people who had gone to prison for leading worship in someone's house instead of going to the state church. When the crops began to fail, Pa and Ma always found ways to stretch the small amount of food they had and invite their poorer neighbors to dinner.

He straightened his shoulders and looked Pa directly in the eyes. "I'm sorry, Pa," he said. He wasn't sure if Pa knew what he was apologizing for, but he felt better.

Pa smiled at Pieter and stood up. He towered over Anna as she stood in the circle of Ma's arms. "You're in good hands, now, Anna," he said. "You were right to trust my children." He took Anna's chin in his big hand and studied her face.

As she gazed back at him, Pieter saw the fear and tension leave her face. The tight, determined look that had been there since he first saw her on the ship melted away. She looked like a little girl for the first time, instead of a tiny adult with too many worries. He breathed a sigh of relief.

"Run and get the hairbrush," Ma said to Elizabeth, "and some water to wash up." She pulled off Anna's dirty cap. "Do you have any clean clothes?" she asked. Anna nodded, and Pieter held out the green traveling bag.

When Elizabeth came back and sat down, Pa paged through the Bible to the New Testament and began to read aloud: "'Love the Lord your God with all your heart and with all your soul and with all your strength and with all your mind'; and, 'Love your neighbor as yourself.' Luke 10, verse 27." He ran his hand through his hair and cleared his throat. "Pieter, Elizabeth, I'm proud and thankful you remembered that today," he said, closing the Bible.

Pieter felt his cheeks burn with pleasure. As Ma brushed and rebraided Anna's hair, he curled up on one of the storage benches, smiling out the window. Helping Anna had been the best thing about the trip since they had left Zeeland.

Chapter Ten

"I see it! I see Grand Haven!" Pieter yelled.

Excitement gripped him as he stood with Elizabeth and Anna and a chattering crowd on the deck of the Great Lakes steamer. It was early morning, with only a pale light in the east stretching above the tops of the dark trees. This was their last stop before they would board a flatboat to take them south down the Lake Michigan coast to Black Lake and the Holland colony.

No one had been able to sleep that night. Everyone was up early. Hollanders, Germans, Yankees—no matter where they were from, Michigan was to be their new home. Some were staying in Grand Haven. Others were going up the Grand River to Grand Rapids.

Pieter heard someone behind him reciting the Lord's Prayer. Others joined in. As they watched the shoreline get closer, the sun rose above the trees and sent shafts of early morning light over them like a benediction. He said a silent thank-you to God that they had made it safely.

Up ahead he could see a small harbor surrounded by high cliffs. Sand dunes topped by dark forests stretched to the north and south as far as he could see.

He focused on the shoreline, searching for Willem in the small crowd that had gathered to meet the steamer. Pa had sent letters ahead from Buffalo, one to Anna's father, the other to Willem, hoping someone would meet them.

Beside Pieter Anna stood quietly, her hands clenched on the rail, her eyes scanning the crowd anxiously. Pieter thought about all they had been through. The huge locks on the Erie

Canal that had raised and lowered the canalboat over the mountains. The long, sometimes boring days when they had practiced their English with the Yankee children who were also moving west. The noise and confusion of the big cities of Buffalo and Detroit.

It seemed forever before they were allowed to disembark. No Willem or Mijnheer De Jong met them as they dragged their belongings up the hill to a ramshackle boardinghouse. As soon as they had eaten breakfast, Neil disappeared to look for Willem. Pa looked at the younger children.

"You might as well go too," he said. "I have business to attend to."

"We'll see if we can find Anna's father," Pieter said. He burst through the door into the main street ahead of Anna and Elizabeth and raced up the dusty road to the next corner.

"Hurry up," he called. "There's so much to see."

Grand Haven was tiny compared to Buffalo or Detroit, but the main street bustled with activity. Men stood at corners arguing in loud voices. Women hurried into the store and out again, baskets filled with supplies. Children played tag in the streets, dodging between the oxen and their watering troughs.

From a blacksmith shop on the corner came the ring of a hammer against iron. Dust tickled Pieter's nose as he pranced about, making him sneeze.

He leaped onto one of dozens of tree stumps that still remained after the trees had been cut down to make room for the stores and houses. More trees, still standing, crowded close to the buildings, casting long shadows into the street.

Next to the blacksmith shop, a store stood tall, its false front rising above the first floor.

"Let's go in," Pieter urged, jumping from the stump and peering through the window. "It's full of stuff. Maybe someone in here knows where Anna's father is."

"We don't have any money to buy anything," Elizabeth said, trying to grab his arm.

47

Pieter pulled away and walked boldly through the door. A bell tinkled above his head. He moved along the aisles lined with barrels of crackers and flour. The fishy smell of herring that hung in the air reminded him of home.

Shelves were stacked high with bolts of cloth, boxes of soap, lanterns, axes, and hammers. People chatted together in the narrow spaces between boxes and barrels. Pieter was proud of himself for understanding most of the words.

Behind the counter, the tallest man he had ever seen poured a dark liquid into a tin cup.

"Name's Payne," he said when he saw Pieter staring at him. "People call me 'The Giraffe.' Want to try some?" Mr. Payne held the cup toward Pieter.

"Yes," he said carefully, instead of "*Ja*." He took a sip of the dark liquid. It was sweet with a tangy flavor.

"What iss it?" he asked in English.

"Root beer," Mr. Payne said.

"Dank you." Pieter finished the root beer and took a deep breath. He thought carefully about the English words he had learned on the canalboat and the steamer.

"We find Mijnheer De Jong," he said. He stopped and corrected himself. "Mister Hendrik De Jong. He lives here." He turned and pointed to Anna and Elizabeth who were peering through the door. "Find Anna's Vader. Father."

Mr. Payne strode to the door. Anna and Elizabeth backed down the steps into the dusty street. Mr. Payne stared at Anna, then turned back to Pieter.

"Hendrik De Jong left to find work south of here," he said. He frowned. "I don't know why he left if he knew his family was on the way here." He sounded as if he didn't like Anna's father very much.

Pieter explained how Anna's mother had died on the ship and how they'd sent a letter. "Maybe he went away before he got the letter," he said.

"Perhaps." Mr. Payne pulled a piece of heavy paper from

behind the counter. "I'll make a sign in case someone knows exactly where he went." He wrote on it in big letters and stuck it in the window so people walking past could read it.

"Someone will tell him his girl is here. Good?" He held out his hand.

"Iss good. Dank you." Pieter shook the hand and nodded.

He left the store, chin up, his shoulders back. Mr. Payne had talked to him as if he were a man, not a child. He had carried on his first real conversation in English in this strange land.

Elizabeth and Anna stood on the steps staring at the poster in the window.

"Why does that sign have my father's name on it?" Anna asked. "Did you find him?"

"No, but don't worry," Pieter said quickly, seeing Anna's lips begin to tremble. "Your father went south. The poster asks anyone who knows where he is to contact Mr. Payne."

"You can come with us to the Holland Colony," Elizabeth said.

Pieter jumped from the steps. "That's right," he said. "Maybe when we get there, your father will be there. And Willem, too." Everything was going to be fine, he was sure of it.

Anna waved through the window at Mr. Payne. "Maybe they will be. Let's go," she said. She trudged back down the dusty street.

They spent the morning exploring the town, then headed back to the boardinghouse.

In the front room Neil sat on a long wooden bench. Pieter opened his mouth to ask when they'd eat, but Neil waved at him to hush. Pa sat at the table, his head in his hands.

Pieter's heart skipped a beat. What was wrong now?

Chapter Eleven

Pieter and the girls slid onto the bench next to Neil.

"What's going on?" Pieter whispered.

"Pa just talked to a family from the Holland Colony," Neil answered. "They're leaving. They say it's full of sick people."

"Do they know Willem?" Pieter asked.

"They think they remember someone named Willem Dekker," Neil said. "They say he staggered out of the woods a few weeks ago, sick with fever. They don't know what happened to him since then."

"Then we have to leave right away." Elizabeth jumped up. "We've got to get to him."

Neil grabbed her arm. "We can't. The owner of the flatboat going to the Holland Colony won't take us without payment. Pa used all our money to get this far. We're stuck without Willem."

Anna gasped. "I have to get to my pa," she said. "He went south somewhere."

Pa rubbed his hands over his face. "We'll see that you're taken care of, Anna," he said. "We'll find someone here for you to stay with until your father is found."

"No!" Pieter said. Anna had to stay with them. How could Pa be so heartless? It was too much. No money meant no food, no tools to work the land, no way to get to Willem, no Anna.

"Does Ma know?" he asked.

Neil nodded. "She's upstairs."

"Perhaps I was wrong in coming here," Pa said. His face sagged. Deep lines ran from the sides of his nose to disappear into his beard. "At least in Zeeland we had a roof over our heads and food to eat."

Pieter pushed past Elizabeth and Anna and out the door. He had to find Ma. He climbed the stairs and knocked on the door of her room.

"Come in," Ma called.

When Pieter opened the door, Ma was sitting in a small chair beneath the window. On the table in front of her were the gold ornaments women wore on their caps on Sundays and holidays. They glittered in the sunshine that fell through the open window.

Two of the ornaments were long pieces of gold wire curled into a spiral shape about three inches long. On the bottom the wire tapered into sharp pins that Ma pushed into the sides of her white cap. The curly pieces stuck out at each side of her forehead. Behind the curly ornaments Ma wore other long stick pins with gold balls fastened to the ends.

Ma picked up one of the pins and turned it in the sunshine. "These were given to me by my grandmother," she said. "She got them from her mother. Women in my family have worn them for years."

She reached for Pieter's hand, then pointed to the dusty street outside the window. "But where would I wear them in this wilderness?" She rubbed her finger along the shiny surface. "They're useless here. We need oxen and tools and seed, not trinkets."

"Are they real gold?" Pieter asked.

"Yes," Ma answered. "They're worth a lot of money. I'd sell them if I could, but your pa would never let me." Her fist clenched around the little gold bauble, and she set it down quickly. Pieter saw a drop of blood where the pin had dug into Ma's palm.

"If only I had learned some English on board ship, I'd sell them before your pa knew anything about it," she said, scrubbing fiercely at the blood on her hand. "But I don't even know who to sell them to." Her eyes filled with tears.

"I know someone who will help," Pieter said, his voice

catching in his throat with excitement. "And I could speak English for you." He told Ma about Mr. Payne—how he had given Pieter root beer, talked to him in English, and made the poster for Anna.

"We can trust him, Ma, I know," he said. "He's not like Mijnheer Van Hout. But what about Pa? He'll be angry." He had never done anything behind Pa's back before, and he was sure Ma never had, either.

"I've always trusted your pa to do what's right," Ma said. "But he's proud. The gold is mine, and he won't like taking what's mine. My grandma would understand, though. Our survival is more important than family treasures."

Her grip tightened on Pieter's hand until it hurt. She rose quickly and wrapped the gold pieces in their cloth covering.

"Come then," she said. She grabbed her shawl and slipped her feet into her shoes. "Let's go before your pa comes upstairs."

An hour later Pieter followed Ma back through the door of the boardinghouse. Her shoes clattered softly on the wood floor as she crossed to Pa and laid some papers and coins on the table in front of him.

Pa stared at Ma, a puzzled look on his face. He picked up the papers, then frowned. "It's in English," he said.

"It's a credit," Pieter said. "From Mr. Payne's store. For food and supplies."

"How—?" Pa looked at Ma in disbelief.

"I sold my gold headpieces," Ma said. She held up her hand, palm out as Pa began to rise. "Sit down, Jan," she said. "There was no reason to keep them. You all forgot I even had them with me. I've talked to a lot of women on the boats since we left Zeeland. Most women sold theirs before they left."

Ma reached up and straightened her cap, pulling it firmly over her ears.

"Pieter helped me sell them," she said, laying her hand on Pieter's shoulder. "He introduced me to Mr. Payne and spoke English for me. You know axes and oxen and flour are necessities, but gold ornaments are not. And if we need more money, there's always my mother's sugar sifter."

"No," Pa said, pushing his chair back and rising to his feet. "You'll not sell that, too. It belonged to your parents. You'll need something to remind you of home." He looked from Ma to Pieter as if he didn't know them anymore.

"We'll sell it if we need to," Ma said in a firm voice. "This is home now." She stood looking calmly at Pa. They faced each other across the table. No one dared to move.

Pieter held his breath. Everything was topsy-turvy in this new world. His quiet, soft-spoken mother had taken charge.

Pa picked up the store credit and put it down again. He rubbed his hand over his eyes, then came around the side of the table and touched Ma lightly on the shoulder.

"You're right, Maatje," he said. "It's a new world. Thank you. Thank you both." He straightened his shoulders. "We'll get the supplies tomorrow and leave as soon as we can." He hesitated, then turned back to Ma. "You had better come to the store with us," he said. "There will probably be many things you'll need that we won't think of."

Ma nodded, then looked over at the rest of them. "Go wash up," she said. "It's almost supper time."

Pieter let out his breath. He followed Neil out to the yard to wash his hands and face. It was a new world, a new way of doing things. Pa was letting others make decisions. Ma was taking charge in ways she never would have dared back in Zeeland.

Pieter splashed water from the bucket on his hands and face. What about his dream of a cabin on the lake? Of running along the shore, fishing in the waters, painting great pictures. Would he have to change his way of thinking, too?

He went back into the boardinghouse and settled at the table with his family. He started to say something to Anna and stopped abruptly. Anna sat with her head down, poking at the beans on her plate.

"Pa?" Pieter asked. "What about Anna?" He told them about

the sign Mr. Payne had placed in his store window.

Pa nodded. "We'll ask everyone around here, see if some-one knows where he went. Anna will come with us. We'll send letters to the towns all around and ask everyone to keep looking for him." He looked at Anna. "Someone will find him. Now that we have money for food and supplies, you can stay with us until he's found."

Anna nodded, her eyes bright with tears. Pieter smiled. They would all be together. They would find Willem. Anna's father would come back. He would buy land next to the Dekkers and they could continue to be friends and neighbors. He accepted a large helping of potatoes from Ma and picked up his fork. He couldn't wait to get to their new home.

Chapter Twelve

A week later Pieter stood in mud so deep his wooden shoes stuck in it. All around him, the small group of Netherlanders that had been with them on the flatboat from Grand Haven huddled together. Pa stood in the center, his lips clamped tightly together.

"Is this it?" Pieter asked. No one answered.

Pieter wondered if everyone else was thinking what he was. Was this the wonderful place God had brought them to? The town was named Holland after a province in the old country, but this was as different from his homeland as he could imagine.

Huge trees, their trunks wider than any Pieter had ever seen, towered overhead. Although it was mid-afternoon, the muddy street ahead was dark. Along its sides he could see log cabins tucked away among the trees. Hundreds of logs lay in stacks alongside the road.

He sloshed through the mud to where Ma sat on a fallen log with Elizabeth. Tears rolled down her cheeks and mixed with the rain that dripped from the leaves overhead.

Anna stood next to her and clutched Ma's hand as if she were afraid Ma would disappear. Elizabeth shivered and pulled her shawl up over her head. What good it would do, Pieter didn't know. They were already covered with mud and wet to the skin from the dangerous journey from Grand Haven.

All along the coast of Lake Michigan as they floated south toward the Holland Colony, the waves had swept into the boat. After they turned east into Black Lake, the winds had calmed, but then they hit the sandbars.

Twice the men had to jump into the water to push the

flatboat when it got stuck. Once they all had to get off and carry their belongings along the shore to the other side of the sandbar. The only thing that kept them going was the knowledge that they were so near their destination.

Through all the rain and mud and cloudy skies, Pa had encouraged them. Pieter had felt a spark of pride to hear Pa singing the Psalms, his deep voice ringing out across the water, slow and steady. Before each scanty meal, Pa prayed, thanking God for bringing them safely to this wonderful new land.

Now Pa looked as discouraged as the rest. "Yes, this is the town of Holland," he said with a sigh. "There's no mistake."

Neil sneezed and wiped his nose with his sleeve, leaving a muddy streak across his face. *We look like ragged tramps,* Pieter thought, worse than any he had seen wandering in New York City or Detroit.

He watched in silence as a tall skinny man strode toward them from a dingy log building on their left. His face was pale and thin and he walked with a limp.

"Welcome to the Holland Colony," he said, shaking hands firmly with each of the men. "Come inside, quickly, and get warm."

He ushered them across the road and into one of the buildings. "You can stay here until you find places of your own," he said. "These cabins were built for newcomers. More and more people arrive every day, as you can see."

The one large room was already crowded. People made way for them, and Pieter pushed in close to the fire that was roaring in the huge fireplace. He heard Ma whisper to Pa, "Ask about Willem."

"My son Willem Dekker is here," Pa said. "And we're looking for this girl's father, Hendrik De Jong. Do you know anything about them?"

The man thought for a moment. "I don't recognize the names, but there are so many sick who came in from the clearings or other villages looking for a doctor. It's possible they're in the town. As soon as you're warm and dry you can look for them." He turned away as another man tugged on his arm.

"He must be here, he must!" Ma said. "We've got to find him, Jan."

Pa took Ma's arm and drew her to a long bench near the fire. Several people got up to make room for them. "We'll find him," he said. "Sit now and rest." He lowered Ma to the bench where she slumped in a heap, her head in her hands.

Was Pa right? Would they ever find Willem? Pieter turned away from the fire. The heat was making the bug bites on his wrists and ankles itch.

The room they were in was low and dark and smelled of damp clothes. Small windows on either side of the door had their shutters thrown back, letting in some dim light. Piles of flour sack mattresses lined the walls. He realized they were all going to have to sleep in this crowded room.

Elizabeth joined him, her eyes red-rimmed from lack of sleep and unshed tears.

"This is horrible," she whispered. "It's worse than being on the ship. Everything here is so dreary." She dragged Pieter to one of the small windows overlooking the swampy street. "If this is the town, what must our clearing be like?" A tear rolled down her cheek. She brushed it away impatiently. "Why didn't that man know Willem? And where's Anna's father?" Her voice shook. "Why did we come here anyway? God can't want us to live in this awful place."

In all the long journey from the old country, Pieter had never seen Elizabeth cry. He felt his own throat close up. He reached out and gripped her hand.

"It will get better, you'll see," he said, not sure he believed it himself. "There must be a reason we're here."

He frowned, struggling for something to say that would make Elizabeth feel better. "Maybe Pa's right," he said. "They didn't want us and our ideas back in the old country. Pa says the *dominies* are free to preach the old ways and beliefs here. No one will try to stop them." He reached down to scratch a mosquito bite on his ankle. What would Elizabeth think of him? He sounded just like Pa.

"You're right," Elizabeth agreed thoughtfully. "More and more people are moving to Michigan every day. Maybe God needs people with strong beliefs like us to start churches here."

Pieter nodded. "There are lots of churches in the old country and on the east coast of America," he said, "but not here." A gust of wind blew the window shutter closed with a bang. He pushed it open again.

"I think the sky is clearing," he said. High above the swaying treetops he could see a tiny patch of blue like a small ray of hope. He turned back to the room as Pa approached.

"You children stay here," he said. "Ma and I are going to look for Willem and Anna's father."

Pieter followed them to the door. "May we go outside?" he asked.

"If you stay near the cabin," Pa answered. He opened the door just as a young man was about to enter from the outside. He was pale with long stringy hair and a scruffy beard. His clothes hung from him like a scarecrow's. He came to a sudden stop when he saw them. Dark circles shadowed bright blue eyes that looked familiar to Pieter.

"Willem!" Pieter shrieked. "It's Willem!" He threw himself at the man, almost knocking him off his feet. Pa reached out and steadied them. The first smile Pieter had seen in weeks spread across Pa's face.

Ma gasped, and the tall man pulled her into his arms. Neil cheered.

Pieter wriggled out from the knot of people as Willem kissed Elizabeth. He couldn't stop smiling. Willem looked tired and his hands shook, but it was Willem, and he was alive. Nothing else mattered.

Willem stepped back to smile at them and bumped into Anna. "Who's this?" he asked.

With a pang of conscience Pieter realized they'd forgotten Anna in their excitement. She stood outside the door, her bag at her feet, looking up the dirt path that led toward the cabins.

"This is Anna De Jong," he said. "Her pa is somewhere near here, but we haven't found him yet." He stopped and whispered, "Her Ma died on the ship."

"Anna De Jong? But—" Willem laid his hand on her shoulder.

"What is it?" Ma asked, coming to Anna's side and taking her hand.

"Is your pa named Hendrik De Jong?" Willem asked.

Anna nodded, her blue eyes wary, her body stiff. *As if she thinks she's going to be hit,* Pieter thought.

"I'm sorry, Anna. There's been a terrible mistake," Willem said. "Your pa received a letter saying that you and your ma both died on board ship. He left the colony a month ago and went farther south. I don't know where."

Anna released her breath in a little spurt. Tears spilled down her cheeks and she began to shake. "What am I going to do now?" she asked. Her body went limp and she sank to the step like a sack of flour.

"You can live with us until we find him. Right, Pa?" Pieter said.

Pa looked at Willem. Willem ran his hands through his long hair. "Of course she can," he said. "One thing I've learned this past year is we all take care of each other. We'll find your father, Anna. Really we will," he said. "We'll send messages to the villages throughout the colony and to the towns south of here."

He took Anna's hand and pulled her from the step. "The sun is out. Let's walk," he said.

Anna held tightly to Willem's hand as if he were a lifeline to her father as they started up the road. Their shoes squelched in the mud as they walked. Everyone tried to talk at once.

Willem told them how a family had taken him in through most of May and June.

"I haven't been back to the clearing since I got the fever," he said. "I was going to leave in a couple of days now that

I'm stronger."

"Now we can all go together," Neil said. He jumped over a log, but his wooden shoes stuck in the mud. He landed on the other side in his stocking feet and let out a yell. Pieter and the others laughed. It felt good to laugh again.

"What's our land like?" he asked, hoping Willem would say it was on Lake Michigan.

"It's not much yet," Willem said, "but it will be a beautiful farm someday." He looked anxiously at Pa. "I know the colony doesn't look like home, but we're free here to talk and discuss and worship as we please."

He told how the leader of the colony, Dominie Van Raalte, had worked tirelessly all year keeping everyone's spirits up and helping hundreds of new immigrants settle in, even when he was sick himself.

"There are villages going up all over the Holland Colony," he said. "You'd be surprised at how many people are in the area already. It's just that this land is so big and the trees so tall, you can't see them." He laughed. "We're starting to build roads and there's even talk of a school soon. We already have a church." He pointed to a road leading southeast from the town.

A school and a church, Pieter thought. "Can we go to church Sunday?" he asked.

Willem shook his head. "We'll have to wait until things are in better shape at the clearing before we can get back for church," he said. "It's already July and my illness put me way behind. We still have to finish the cabin and put the roof on."

"There's a cabin already?" Ma asked in surprise.

"Partly," Willem said. "Some friends helped before I got sick. But I'm worried about my potatoes and corn. The animals have probably eaten them. We'll have to replant. You brought money and supplies?" he asked Pa.

Pieter waited for Pa to tell Willem to stop making decisions for him and ordering them around. Instead, Pa told Willem how Pieter and Ma had sold Ma's cap ornaments for food and supplies. "We have everything we need for the summer," he said. "But very little money is left."

"We'll need some of it to rent an ox," Willem said. "We'll never get our supplies to the clearing otherwise. Or get the rest of the cabin up."

Pa pulled a piece of paper from his pocket and began marking figures on it. "There won't be much left," he said. "But we still have your wages from working for Mr. Carter last winter," he said to Willem.

Willem shook his head. "There are no wages, Pa," he said. "Mr. Carter got sick and died before he could pay me. His wife moved back to New York State to be with her family." He kicked at some pine cones on the ground. "She had no money to pay me, so she left me twenty acres of land instead."

"Could we sell it?" Pa asked.

"Perhaps, but I haven't located it yet," Willem said. "She said it's somewhere in the vicinity of our property. The papers with the exact coordinates haven't arrived from the land office yet." He looked Pa straight in the eyes, and Pieter realized that Willem had grown as tall as Pa.

Pa put his hand on Willem's shoulder. "We're all together again," he said. "That's all that's important. We don't need money. We have each other."

"Let's go back and get some rest," Ma said. She took Pa's hand, something Pieter had rarely seen her do, then reached out and stroked Anna's sad face. "We're a family again, and we're your family now until we find your father. Let's get ready to leave."

Chapter Thirteen

Three days later Pieter and his family left the town of Holland and headed southwest. There was no room on the narrow trail for a wagon, so a sturdy ox plodded alongside them. It was piled high with boxes, axes, hoes, chains and ropes, and bags of flour, potatoes, and corn. Pa, Willem, and Neil walked ahead. Ma and the girls brought up the rear. Pieter alternated between running ahead and trudging behind the ox.

The Indian trail they followed was barely wide enough for the ox. Tall oaks and maples arched overhead, blocking out the sun. Their wooden shoes slipped in the mud.

"How long will it take?" Pieter asked, jumping over a pool of dirty water.

"Probably most of the day," Pa said. "Especially since we'll have to rest often. Especially Willem."

Pieter sighed. He hadn't had so much as a glimpse of the lake along the trail. The trees were too thick. He knew their clearing was in the dense woods, Willem had said so. But Willem had also said their clearing was southwest of Holland. And wasn't that closer to Lake Michigan? He had been so sure they'd see the lake through the trees. Then he would always know it was there waiting for him.

Elizabeth and Anna lagged behind to pick wildflowers along the edge of the trail. The ox grunted. Sparrows twittered cheerfully in the bushes. Pieter trudged on. At noontime they stopped for lunch. Twice they forded small streams. The ox slipped in the mud at one, but with everyone pushing and pulling, they got it up the low bank to the other side.

It was late in the afternoon when Willem stopped at a narrow path leading off to the right. "We'll have to take some of the baggage off the ox and carry it," he said. "This path is narrower than the trail. It'll take us at least two trips to get everything to the clearing."

Pieter was left with Anna and the boxes of clothes and bedding while Pa and the boys pushed and prodded the ox through the trees. Elizabeth and Ma carried boxes and baskets.

Pieter sat and listened for the sound of the lake, but heard nothing, only the restless sighing of the trees. Sunshine dappled with shadows flickered across Anna's face.

"My pa will never find me here," she said. She sat on a large rock at the edge of the trail, her chin in her hands.

"We left word with everyone in Holland. Pa sent letters to Allegan and Kalamazoo. Someone will find him." Pieter sat next to her and picked up some small stones. He tossed them idly into the woods. A squirrel burst out of the bushes and up a tree, his tail flicking angrily, making Pieter jump.

Anna sighed. "I guess. You don't know my pa. He might be hundreds of miles away by now."

They sat, not saying much, until Pa and the boys returned with the ox and loaded the rest of their belongings. Neil went ahead holding back tree branches. Pieter came behind with Anna. He saw a patch of sky up ahead, and suddenly they were out of the trees and into the open.

The sun was already dropping behind the trees and the clearing was in shadow. Pieter saw tree stumps sitting like fat little men all over the ground. Huge tree trunks lay beside many of them.

In the middle of the clearing a partially built house, its walls about three feet high, stood open to the sky. Branches covered with leaves and bark leaned against one wall to form a small shelter. On all sides of the clearing trees crowded close.

There was no lake to be seen. Pieter swallowed hard as disappointment rose in his throat.

"First thing we have to do is finish the cabin," Willem said.

"Ma and the girls can use the shanty until then."

They moved across the clearing to the log building Willem called the shanty. It was about eight feet long and six feet wide with a low door cut into the front. Around the shanty and the cabin, the larger trees had been cleared away. In between and all around the tree stumps, Willem had planted corn and potatoes.

Pieter remembered Ma's beautiful garden at home in Zeeland. The brightly colored tulips, the neat rows of vegetables, the brilliant blue of the sky overhead. This patch of land was like a common toad in comparison. How could he ever paint beautiful pictures in this ugly place?

"I helped friends build their cabins and they helped me start this one before the fever hit," Willem said. "Then people began to get sick. I tried to keep going, but . . ." His voice trailed off. "Now that you're here, we'll have this place finished in no time." He turned back to the ox. "Let's get unloaded."

Pieter watched in surprise as Pa picked up a trunk. Why was Pa taking orders from Willem? Then he realized that Pa didn't know what to do any more than he did. Pa had been a farmer in the Netherlands, but farming in Michigan was completely different.

He headed for the shanty. He would take a look inside, then find a tree stump to sit on. He would draw a picture of the clearing to send to Dirk. He had written one letter that had been sent back with some folks in Albany who were going back to Zeeland. Last week he had started another. He could finish the letter and maybe Neil would take it to town to mail.

"Pieter!" Pa's sharp voice stopped him. "Get back here and help unload."

He felt his cheeks redden. Anna and Elizabeth were sorting through the boxes looking for blankets. He picked up the end of a small trunk and helped Neil carry it between the tree stumps. They set it down outside the door of the shanty.

"We'll unpack only what we need for now," Willem said as

he ducked through the door. "There's not much room," he added apologetically to Ma.

Pieter crowded in behind Willem. The shanty had no windows. In the dim light from the doorway, he saw a log platform built close to the ground. It stretched from the front to the back on one side of the small enclosure. A dirty mattress covered the platform.

On the other side of the doorway two small shelves had been built over a broad waist-high workspace. Some pegs for clothes had been hammered into the wall between the bed and the shelves. The floor was dirt.

"Do I have to sleep on the dirt?" he asked, wrinkling his nose.

"You'll not be sleeping in here," Pa said from the doorway. "This is for Ma and the girls. You'll sleep in the lean-to with the rest of us."

Pieter straightened his shoulders. Of course, there was only room in the shanty for the girls and Ma. He would sleep outside with the men. But when he looked out at the tall forest surrounding the tiny clearing, he shuddered. He didn't think he would sleep for a minute under those great trees.

But he was wrong. By the time darkness made it too difficult to do any more work, Pieter was so exhausted he thought he could sleep anywhere. He took the blanket Ma gave him, curled up on a patch of leaves, and was soon asleep.

Chapter Fourteen

The sky was just beginning to get light when Pieter felt his shoulder shaken.

"Get up. There's work to be done," Pa said. "Ma has breakfast ready."

Pieter staggered out of the lean-to and splashed water from a pail over his hands and face. Breakfast was laid out on a log stretched across two tree stumps. He took a slice of bread with maple sugar from Ma. Willem and Pa organized the work over breakfast.

"I'll show Pa and Neil how to cut down the trees the way I learned from the Americans." Willem brought out three axes and set them on the table. "Then I'll chop the smaller branches off the logs that have already been cut. I wish I could do more. Everyone is to stay safely on this side of the clearing until you get used to the way the trees fall. We don't want anyone hurt."

Willem picked up an ax. "Pieter, as soon as I've cut the smaller branches off the tree trunks, you'll drag them to that pile of brush over there."

Pieter's glance swept across the clearing. It was ugly with those squat stumps and huge piles of brush between the hated trees.

"I can't do that," he said. "The branches are too big and scratchy. I'll help Ma." He turned to go into the shanty.

"You'll do as you're told," Pa said. "We need every available body to clear this land. Or do you want your brother to get sick again from working too hard?" He picked up an ax and followed Willem to the tall trees ringing the clearing.

No, I don't want Willem sick again, Pieter thought. *But I don't want to chop trees either.* Why couldn't they at least live in town? He never would have been expected to work back in Zeeland. He could have continued to go to school and maybe even to the university. He could have become a great artist like Rembrandt. None of that could happen now. It would take the rest of their lives to chop down all these trees.

Once Pa and Neil were at work on the other side of the clearing, Willem motioned to Pieter. Pieter followed, hoping Ma would stop him. But Ma said nothing. He grabbed a branch as Willem swung the ax and chopped at one of the fallen trees. Pieter dragged the branch across the yard, flinging it with all his strength onto the pile of underbrush.

He yanked at another branch before Willem had chopped it all the way through. He stomped away with it, ignoring Willem's caution to slow down. All morning he clumped back and forth, his wooden shoes wearing a path to the brush pile. At dinnertime he ate without speaking to anyone, then went back to work. He worked until his shoulders ached and his palms were raw from the rough bark of the tree limbs.

Slowly his anger seeped away, and he concentrated on making the pile as high as he could. Behind him he heard the clang of axes on wood. He looked up only when he heard Neil shout, just to make sure the falling trees were not crashing in his direction.

By the time Pa called to them to quit, he could only stagger toward the supper Ma had set out. He collapsed to the ground and closed his eyes, then leaped up with a yell as water from a dipper splashed over his hot face.

"Come on, lazybones," Neil said. "We're going swimming."

"Don't be ridiculous." Pieter felt as growly as a hungry bear.

"Go on," Ma laughed. "You'll be surprised." Willem was disappearing down a dark path that led into the trees behind the shanty.

Pieter ran to catch up. His breath caught in his throat as the trees closed over his head. It was dark in the woods. He heard

Willem yell up ahead, and then the sound of splashing. He
burst into a small clearing where the light was brighter. Willem
splashed in a pool shadowed by tree limbs. Neil dashed past,
kicked off his wooden shoes, and hurtled into the water. Pieter
followed him, wading in without taking his clothes off.

The water came only to his chest, and it was cold, but it
soothed his aching muscles. He ducked all the way under,
holding his breath as long as he could, then rose to the surface, sending ripples across the pond.

Neil hung by his hands from a low overhanging branch.
He kicked up a spray of water and sent it over his brothers.
Pieter splashed back. Neil lost his grip and plunged into the
water. He came up spluttering.

"There are fish in here, Pieter," he called. "We could go
fishing after work tomorrow."

"Yes, let's." Pieter rolled over on his back and floated. His
clothes pulled him under, and he surfaced to hear the clanging
of a bell. For a moment he thought he was back in Zeeland.

But something was different here besides the pines and
maples above his head and the darkening water. As he
reached the edge of the pool, Neil reached back and
extended his hand, pulling him up the bank.

That's it, he thought. *That's what's different. First the
work, then the swim.* All afternoon he'd been working with
his brothers. Working as hard as they had. In the old country
they would never have included him in their fun. He followed
them back up the path, marveling at how quickly things had
changed in only four months. And not all for the worst.

After stuffing himself with potatoes at supper, he got his
blanket and curled up in the lean-to. He felt the ominous pres-
ence of the trees above him, but the soft voices of his family and
the darkness itself seemed to hold them at bay. Stars sparkled in
the patch of sky he could see between the branches of the shelter. An owl hooted in the distance. His eyes closed.

"Ma made a mattress with some flour sacks and leaves," he

heard Willem say to Neil. "We could draw straws for it."

"No drawing straws," came Pa's quiet voice. "Let Pieter have it. He's earned it."

Someone slapped the mattress onto the ground and rolled Pieter onto it. Just before he fell asleep, his tired brain registered Pa's words of praise.

During the night the wind rose. Thunder rumbled in the distance, waking Pieter, then sounded closer, long rolling waves of sound. Lightning lit up the swaying trees. He grabbed his mattress and dashed for the shanty with Pa and the boys just as the rains came. He crashed through the door, stumbled over Elizabeth and Anna, and crouched in a corner with his arms covering his head.

Thunder roared overhead like twenty cannons going off at once. Pa and the older boys crowded through the door soaking wet. The shed was wall to wall people. The rain hit the outside boards in sheets of water and poured down the sides. The roof began to leak, sending a trickle of water onto Pieter's head. He moved closer to Willem.

Anna began to cry and Ma pulled her and Elizabeth close. Neil's breath whistled in Pieter's ear. More thunder boomed. Somewhere in the woods a tree crashed to the ground. Pieter was sure the next one would fall on the shanty, killing them all. Willem put his arm around him and Pieter shivered against him. Pa began to recite the Twenty-third Psalm.

For what seemed like hours, thunder boomed and lightning flashed between the cracks in the walls of the shed. Then slowly the storm moved off. The lightning stopped. The thunder rumbled distantly.

For a long time no one moved, then Willem said in a shaky voice, "Well, that was a bad one. We'd better work fast to get the cabin finished. There will be more storms like this throughout the summer."

Chapter Fifteen

Throughout the remainder of July and into August, Pieter worked beside his brothers. He knew grumbling was no good. Every hand was needed, but he wished he were somewhere else. Somewhere out in the bright sunshine with Sep and his drawing tools.

While he and Willem cleared the limbs from the trees, Neil and Pa cut the trunks into twelve foot lengths for the smaller ends of the cabin. Taller trees were cut for the longer sides. Then Pa and Willem hooked the logs to the ox with heavy chains. The huge beast pulled the logs to the level area in the middle of the clearing where the cabin stood.

Willem notched the ends of the logs, and Pa and Neil hooked each one to the ox. With the ox pulling and Pa and Neil steadying the log, they positioned each one on top of the others to form the walls.

Once a log came loose and crashed to the ground, barely missing Pa. After that, Ma fussed so much that they quit when the walls were only about Pa's height. Even with everyone's help the logs were too heavy to lift much higher. Pa and Willem would have to be careful not to bump their heads on the rafters.

The roof would be thatched with bark, and no window or chimney openings were cut yet, but it was bigger than the shanty, and they could all sleep inside. Ma would cook outside as long as the weather was good.

Ma, Elizabeth, and Anna tended the potatoes and corn. Ma planted beans and squash at the bottom of the stalks of corn the way Willem said the Indians did. Anna and Elizabeth chased the birds and deer away from the crops and pulled weeds. They searched for berries in the woods, always staying close to the creek that flowed from the swimming hole so they wouldn't get lost in the woods.

One day Pa brought Pieter an ax. "We need more under-brush cleared away," he said. "Clear away the vines and chop down the thick bushes and saplings." He showed him how to swing the ax.

Anna and Elizabeth and sometimes Ma helped drag the underbrush to piles. Not once had Pieter had time to do anything except work.

One day, Neil got up earlier than usual and left the clearing. "Where's he going?" Pieter asked.

"To town," Pa said. "To see if there's mail."

Pieter picked up his bread and reached for the maple sugar. He wished they had a couple of hens so they could have eggs once in a while. Or a cow for milk. He was tired of bread. He couldn't remember the last time he'd had a cup of milk. Even when the cabin was finished and they could sit inside for a change, the bread didn't taste any better.

That night Neil returned, grinning from ear to ear. He pulled something from his pocket.

Letters! Neil handed one to Pa, one to Willem, and held a third above his head. "Guess who this one's for?" he said.

"Me!" Pieter lunged at Neil and grabbed his arm.

Neil laughed and handed him the letter. "You're right, little brother, it's for you. Will you read it to us?"

"Later," Pieter said. He crossed the clearing to his favorite stump, holding the letter tenderly as if it would break like glass if he dropped it. He took a deep breath and slit the edge carefully.

> Dear Pieter,
>
> I received your letter from Albany. All is well here although Sep and I were lonely for awhile without you. We are now best friends. Sep is fine and healthy. He is going to be a father. My

sister Gertie's dog will have puppies soon. Sep
caught three rabbits and found one of our
calves that strayed into a ditch. Father says he's
a good watchdog. Father also says many people
are leaving Zeeland to go to America. I will send
this letter with someone going to Michigan. I
wish I were having adventures like you. It is
very boring here. It will be worse when school
starts and you won't be here to help me with
my numbers. How do you like Michigan? Are
there bears and wolves?

Your friend,
Dirk

Dirk bored? With Sep to play with and school to go to? *I
wish I could be bored for only a day,* Pieter thought. *Just
one day with nothing to do, that's all I want. A day to play
instead of work.* A pang of sadness settled in his stomach as
he thought of the fun he and Dirk used to have with Sep.
Would he ever have time for fun again?

He tucked the letter in his pocket. At least Sep was happy.
He pictured Sep as a father, with puppies clamoring all over
him. He knew now that Sep was better off with Dirk. He
never would have survived the trip cooped up in a crate. He
would have died of unhappiness. He returned to the others in
time to hear Willem reading a letter aloud.

"Range. Section. Hmm-mm," Willem murmured. He
scratched his nose. "That's not too far west of here."

"What is?" Pieter asked.

"The twenty acres Mrs. Carter left me," Willem answered. "I
finally received a letter giving me the coordinates. She told
me there's a half-built cabin on it and a stream runs through
the property. It might even be Bark Creek, the same one that
runs through our land. Maybe next year we'll have time to go

look for it." He put the letter on the shelf he had made above the row of pegs for their clothes.

Somewhere to the west, Pieter thought. Closer to the lake. He sighed. He would never see the lake again, he was sure. Even if there were a road to follow west, which there wasn't, there was no time to go look, either for Willem's property or the lake.

He listened half-heartedly to Grandma's letter from Goes and went to bed feeling even more tired than he normally did.

Chapter Sixteen

The clattering of pots and pans woke Pieter early one Sunday morning. It was still dark, but Ma was already up. He crawled out of his blankets and stumbled to the outhouse in the woods.

When he returned, Anna and Elizabeth were up, too, bringing dishes to the long board they used as a table.

"Come help us, Pieter," Ma called. "We need to eat quickly and pack our lunch."

Pieter yawned and reached to take a pile of plates from Anna. "Just think," he said. "We're finally going to church."

The roof of the cabin was thatched. An opening had been cut in one wall, and Pa and Neil had piled a huge collection of stones ready to build the chimney. Willem had felt strong enough to walk into town and return the ox to its owner so someone else could use it. Pa had decided that from now on, they would walk to church every Sunday.

This time the walk went faster than when they had first walked the trail. *A month ago,* Pieter thought. *How much has changed.* The summer heat had dried the mud and they had no ox to slow them down. Neil whistled cheerfully until Pa frowned at him. It was Sunday, after all.

Ma had done her best to patch their worn clothes and bleach the girls' caps in the sun. Pieter didn't care that his shirt was too small and had patches on the elbows. He skipped happily behind his family so Pa wouldn't see him kicking stones. Suddenly he heard voices.

Two men appeared from a path at the side of the trail. They wore the dark trousers and black waistcoat and shirt of Zeeland. Pa stopped to greet them. Five minutes later a family appeared from another path. They, too, were dressed like the others, and the men had the same black cloth hats with the rolled brims as Pa and Willem wore.

By the time the sun was fully up, the trail streamed with people on their way to the church.

"Where did you all come from?" Pieter asked a boy who introduced himself as Kees.

Kees laughed. "We live all over the woods. There are clearings everywhere." He looked curiously at Pieter. "Is this your first time going to church?"

"Yes, we haven't had time before," Pieter answered. Maybe Kees would think they were heathens for not going to church.

"I know," Kees said. "There's so much to be done if you're new. But it's wonderful to get together. Sometimes we have the services outdoors like we did last summer. Even though we have a church building now." He picked up a stone and threw it into the woods.

Pieter hoped it would be one of those days they sat outdoors. Michigan had so many gloomy, cloudy days, he wanted to enjoy every bit of sunshine he could.

By the time they reached the churchyard, they had picked up the townspeople as well, and left behind an empty town. Although the women's dresses were patched and faded and many of the men came in work pants and shirts, Pieter could tell by their clothes that the settlers had originally come from all over the Netherlands, not just Zeeland.

They chattered together like squirrels as they settled onto the logs laid out alongside the cemetery at one side of the new church building.

When Dominie Van Raalte rose to take his place behind a tree stump used as a pulpit, a hush spread over the crowd. It felt like years, not just months, since Pieter had been in church. He bowed his head in silence with the others.

After the *dominie's* greeting and the opening prayer, the *voorzanger*, the song leader, stood up and announced the first song. People opened their psalm books to the ninety-sixth psalm. Pieter listened to the slow solemn notes as the voices rose in song, strong and pure up through the trees.

"Worship the Lord in the splendor of his holiness; tremble before him, all the earth."

Ma poked him in the ribs with her elbow, and he joined in.

"Say among the nations, 'The Lord reigns.' The world is firmly established, it cannot be moved . . ." he sang.

That is true, he thought. He was halfway around the world from home, but home was still there. Sep and Dirk were still there. The world was firmly established, and so was he. Established here in this wilderness.

Would he ever see anything but trees around him again? He hadn't even known all these people lived here. He tried to block out his dark thoughts and concentrate on the psalm.

> Let the heavens rejoice, let the earth be glad,
> let the sea resound, and all that is in it;
> let the fields be jubilant, and everything in them.
> Then all the trees of the forest will sing for joy;
> they will sing before the Lord, for he comes,
> he comes to judge the earth.

The song ended. Dominie Van Raalte bowed his head to pray.

The psalm was just like poetry. Pieter's thoughts strayed from the long prayer. He remembered the power of the sea. The brightness of the heavens on a cloudless day or star-filled night. Yes, they could resound with gladness.

Someday the cleared fields would be jubilant with corn and wheat. But he couldn't imagine the trees singing with joy. Only howling on windy nights, or crashing in storms or under the ax. Or worse, making no sounds at all, just standing like soldiers, tall and threatening, imprisoning him in their small clearing.

He sneaked a look at the churchyard beneath half-closed eyelids. Sun glanced off the walls of the new church. *At least the trees provide us with shelter once they're cut down,* he thought. *And some are beautiful, like the plum tree on the other side of our pond. I could paint a picture of it if I had paints.*

Through the long three-hour service, as he squirmed on the log bench, he drew pictures in his head. Pictures swarming with color. Pictures of Zeeland, of Sep and Dirk. Pictures of Lake Michigan with white billowy clouds above and the sun sparkling off the water. He longed to be able to look out and see nothing but endless skies and blue-green water.

By the time the final psalm was sung, Anna was drowsing on Ma's shoulder, and Pieter could hardly keep his eyes open. He was glad the *dominie* didn't know them yet, or he might have called out their names the way he had when one of the tired farmers fell asleep in the middle of the sermon.

As he stretched his tired legs and rubbed his sore bottom, the men gathered to talk over the sermon and smoke their pipes. Anna and Elizabeth joined the other girls playing with the babies.

Pieter saw Kees beckoning from the side of the church building and ran to join him.

"I know we're not supposed to play on Sunday," Kees said. He led Pieter behind the church to a group of boys waiting at the top of a hill. "But sometimes we can get a few races in before the elders stop us."

Pieter lost most of the races down to the stream and back up the hill, but he didn't care. When the clanging of a bell announced lunch, he was tired and happy. He took his bread back to the group of boys and listened to their chatter.

Most of them were just as thin and scraggly as he was, with uncut hair, and wrists and ankles that stuck out of outgrown clothes. One boy was a bit plumper than the rest.

"We have a cow, and milk every day," he bragged until Kees tackled him and made him stop.

After lunch they had another service. This one was shorter,

but it was even harder to stay awake. Then everyone packed up and began to drift away. As they headed up the road through town, many of Pieter's new friends dropped away. He and Kees waved good-bye and headed with the other farm families down the Indian trail that led back into the forest.

It wasn't true what he had thought during the *dominie's* long prayer. The trees weren't always menacing. They provided shelter and fuel for the fireplace. They dropped nuts to gather, and the rabbits and deer sheltering in the woods would give them food for the long winter months.

They couldn't hold him prisoner, either, he realized. The trail that led to their clearing led to other cabins too. At the end was the town with its church, and maybe someday, before he was too old to go, there would be a school.

There was Bark Creek, running west from the pool through their land and beyond. *Running toward the lake,* Pieter thought. He would not let the trees hold him prisoner. Somehow, some way, even if it were ten miles, even if it took days, he'd follow that creek all the way to Lake Michigan.

Chapter Seventeen

"May I have that?" Pieter asked.

Ma finished unwrapping the sausages Willem had brought from town and held out the paper to Pieter. Grease spotted it on one side.

"Another letter?" she asked.

"No." Pieter turned the paper over and smoothed out the unspotted side. "I thought maybe I could use it for drawing or painting."

Pa frowned. "Not today," he said. He placed his coffee mug on his plate and handed them to Elizabeth. "You've got to get rid of the weeds around the vegetables today."

"You can't paint pictures without paint, anyway," said Neil.

"I've got some ideas for making paints," Pieter said. "There are still some berries in the woods, and that dark clay near the pond would . . ."

"Pieter," Pa interrupted. "What did I tell you to do?"

"Yes, Pa." Pieter gave Anna his plate and cup. He had so many drawings in his book, he wanted to put them together in a larger picture.

He could see the scene in his head. The quiet green countryside of Zeeland, a windmill next to a canal, its wide blades stretched to meet the clouds. Only one tree and the stretch of the blue sky above. Sep running alongside the water. When would he ever get any time to do what he wanted? All he did was work, work, work.

He sighed, then folded the paper and put it in his pocket. He followed Pa and his brothers out to the clearing and picked up the hoe.

He chopped at the weeds, being careful not to hurt Ma's bean plants. Along the edge of the vegetable patch he saw some small blue flowers nestled in the grass.

He set down the hoe and looked across the clearing. Pa and Willem were hidden by the cabin. He didn't know where Neil was. He pulled the paper from his pocket.

The flowers were the exact shade of the Zeeland sky. If he crushed them and added a drop of water, he might be able to make something like paint that could be smeared across the paper. The yellow daisies growing in a patch of sun next to the pond would be just the right shade for Sep's coat when mixed with a little clay.

He sneaked one more look around to see if Pa were watching, then snatched a handful of the blue flowers and ducked beneath the trees.

At the pond he found a few large leaves to hold water. He took out his charcoal sticks and sketched a rough outline of the Zeeland landscape. He had drawn Sep so often over the past four months that it took only a few minutes to complete the drawing.

When the drawing was done, he gently tore a small section off the side of the paper. He crushed a few of the blue flowers onto the paper, then dribbled a tiny bit of water over them. With a small twig he brushed the blue color across the paper.

He worked steadily. The sky was streaky and he couldn't quite get the color of Sep's coat right, but the grass looked as fresh as he remembered and the windmill stood tall above the canal. His first painting! He felt sure it was only one of many more he would do.

"Pieter!"

Pieter leaped to his feet. The painting fluttered to the ground. His pencils and book spilled from his lap.

"What are you doing here?" Pa's body was rigid, his fists clenched. "How dare you disobey and sneak off when there's work to be done." He bent and picked up Pieter's book and pencils.

"I'll keep these," he said, his voice tight with anger. "This is

Michigan, Pieter, not Zeeland. If we want to get through the winter, we have to work. There's no time for play."

"No, Pa, please," Pieter cried. "Please let me keep them. It's not play, it's important. I promise. I won't run off again. Please, just let me keep my book."

"Not until you've shown me you can get through a day without thinking only of yourself. There are other people in this family depending on you." Pa put the pencils and book in his deep trouser pocket. "Come along, now," he said.

"My picture!" Pieter reached for his painting, but Pa grabbed the collar of his shirt and jerked him upright.

"Leave it," he said. He marched Pieter back up the path. "Pictures are for people who have time and money to enjoy them. We have neither."

Pieter stumbled up the path in front of Pa. His painting would be ruined left lying by the pond. The dampness would make the colors run and wash away his reminder of home. Tears blinded his eyes. He was already beginning to forget what Zeeland looked like. All he seemed to see lately when he closed his eyes were the hateful clearing and the tall trees closing in around it.

He hated America. He wished they'd never come. At least in the old country Pa had left him alone, even if he didn't like him spending so much time drawing and daydreaming. In Zeeland Pa hadn't hated art, either. He remembered the beautiful painting of the windmill that hung on the wall at home and the blue and white tiles that lined the mantelpiece. Pa had bought the painting and hung it himself. Now all he thought about was work.

Pieter tripped on a tree root. "Pa," he tried again, but Pa interrupted him as they reached the edge of the woods.

"I want to see that bean patch free of every weed by noon. And after lunch, you'll stack wood until supper time." Pa handed Pieter the hoe. "If you can't understand that we'll starve or freeze this winter if we don't work now, maybe this will teach you. Now get to work."

Pieter turned his back on Pa and whacked at the nearest weed. *So what if we starve,* he thought. *I hate it here anyway. Why did we have to come? All we do is work and go to church on Sunday.* Was being able to worship the way they wanted so important that they didn't have time for anything but work?

He sighed and tossed a weed to the side of the vegetable patch. He knew the answer, but anger still burned at the back of his mind. Pa didn't have to be so mean about his picture. That's what this country did to you. It turned you mean. Pa had never been jolly, but he'd never been mean before, either.

He wondered if he dared to sneak back and get his painting, but the thought of Pa's anger stopped him. He'd have to wait until after supper. By then it would be dark. He shuddered at the thought of going through the woods in the dark, but he would do it for his painting. He'd hide it someplace where Pa wouldn't find it.

He pulled weeds and stacked wood all day. On the way to the outhouse just before bedtime, he detoured up the path to the pond. His heart thumped as an owl called and some nighttime animal rustled the bushes on his left. The moon passed in and out of the clouds making shadows move across the path ahead of him.

When he reached the pond, he went straight to the spot where he had dropped the painting. There was nothing there. He walked in ever widening circles around the spot, searching the ground carefully. Had it blown into the pond? No, he had been too far from the pond. Besides, there hadn't been any wind.

When he thought Ma would begin to wonder where he was, he trudged back to the cabin, his heart heavy in his chest. His painting was gone. He'd never be able to do another one. By the time he had the chance, he knew he wouldn't remember what Zeeland looked like anymore.

Chapter Eighteen

After the day he lost his painting, Pieter lost track of time. Nothing seemed to matter anymore. At night he fell into bed, too exhausted to care that Pa still had his drawing book. None of their new friends from church stopped by to interrupt the monotony of their days. Every family was too busy getting ready for winter.

Then one day Pieter heard the whinny of a horse coming from the direction of the path. He watched a tall man on a chestnut mare *clip-clop* his way out of the trees toward the clearing.

"Hello," the man called. He reined in his horse and swung down from the saddle. "I wonder if you could help me. I'm looking for—"

"Pa!" a voice screamed behind Pieter. He whirled to see Anna flying across the yard, her apron flapping. The bucket she carried clattered to the ground.

"Anna!" the man shouted as Anna dashed past Pieter and flung herself into the man's arms. "I thought I'd never see you again." Tears streamed down his face as he swung Anna up in his arms, twirling about the yard with her.

Pieter watched in amazement. The man set Anna down and held her away from him. Then he took her hands and began to dance around the yard, swinging her in circles. Anna laughed and tried to get him to stop so she could hug him again.

Ma came from around the side of the house where she had been doing laundry. Elizabeth followed. They stood staring at the wild man in front of them. Anna's father stopped dancing when he saw Ma. He scooped Anna up in his arms again as if she were three years old and advanced on Ma with his hand out, a big grin on his face.

Ma wiped her hands on her apron and shook his hand. She kissed Anna on the cheek.

"Come into the house," she said.

Pieter's cheeks hurt from smiling at Anna and her strange, boisterous father. Here was the father he had always wished he had. Jolly, laughing, talking, enfolding Anna in warm hugs. Pa walked in, quiet as always, his smile polite. He shook hands with Mijnheer De Jong, his glance darting to Ma's face.

Watching Anna's rosy cheeks as she sat on her father's lap, Pieter thought he'd never seen her so happy. Then an unpleasant thought hit him. Anna would be leaving them now. She would go to live with her father. His face stiffened as he tried to keep smiling for Anna's sake, but what would they do without her? She was like a sister to them. He went to stand next to Elizabeth.

"How'd you find me, Pa? Where were you?" Anna bounced off her father's lap and sat next to him on the bench. He put his arm around her and she snuggled close to his side. Pieter ached with envy. Even Ma didn't hug him like that anymore.

"When I heard that you and your ma had died on the ship, I was devastated," Mijnheer De Jong said. "So I packed up and moved south. There's a lot of work to be had all over Michigan. Then I got a letter from a friend in California. He says they've found gold there. I came back to the colony to sell my land a couple of days ago, so I could go join him in California."

His arm tightened around Anna. "The minute I heard about you, I left to find you. Someone there told me a fine family had taken you in." He reached out and took Ma's hand. "I thank you from the bottom of my heart for taking care of my little girl."

"Now you won't have to sell your land," Anna said. "We can set up a house together. You look like you need someone to take care of you." She pointed to the front of her father's shirt, which was missing a button.

Mijnheer De Jong laughed and rose from the bench to greet

84

Neil who had burst through the door, face and hands scrubbed for dinner. Ma picked up a knife and began to cut thick slices of bread. Pieter went outside to wash his hands. How soon would Anna and her father leave? If Mijnheer De Jong's land was nearby, then he and Anna would be neighbors. They could visit often. Maybe they could go to school together.

As Mijnheer De Jong chattered happily about California while they ate, Pieter became aware of a stillness in the room. Ma pushed her plate away. Pa ate silently, not looking at anyone. Anna's face had gone very still, the rosy glow faded. As soon as she had helped clear the table, she slipped out the door. Pieter followed. From behind him he heard Neil laugh at something Mijnheer De Jong said.

Anna settled on a stump at the edge of the clearing. Pieter sat on the ground in front of her. "What's the matter?" he asked.

"It's Pa." Anna twisted her hands in her apron. She swallowed hard. "I thought he'd be changed."

"Changed?" Pieter asked. He liked Anna's father the way he was. "Why do you want him changed?"

Anna sighed and smoothed out her apron. "We never stay in one place," she said. "Even in Holland Pa kept moving from job to job. There was always something better somewhere else."

"But now he owns land here." Pieter picked up a twig from the ground and chewed on it. "Now that he's found you, he'll settle down."

Anna shook her head. "You heard him. He's already talking about California. That's way across the country. I like it here. I dreamed so long about living in a house of our own. Me and Pa and Ma. Now—" She choked on her words. "Now we'll move again. I know we will."

She looked back at the cabin just as her father came through the door. He waved. Anna drew in a deep breath. "At least I've got my pa back. That's most important. I'll write you lots of letters from wherever we live." She jumped up and raced back to the house.

Letters. Pieter thought about Dirk's letter. He had only had one in four months. It took so long for letters to cross the ocean. It would take a long time for a letter to go all the way from California to Michigan, too.

Why did people have to keep moving about? First Pieter's family. Now Anna. *I'll lose another friend,* he thought gloomily. *No one ever seems to want to stay in one place.*

Chapter Nineteen

Anna and her father did not leave. Mijnheer De Jong stayed to help Pa and the boys. They raised the walls of the cabin, cut windows, and finished the fireplace and chimney. Then they built a loft and rethatched the roof.

"Next we'll chink the cracks in the house," Willem said. "Breezes blowing through your house are fine in August, but won't be so pleasant when winter comes." As the fresh wood of the cabin had dried and shrunk, wide cracks appeared between the logs in the walls. They filled them with a mixture of leaves and twigs, then plastered the walls with clay inside and out.

All through August Anna and her father stayed. One day he rode off, saying he needed to do business in Allegan.

"He'll come back," Pieter assured Anna.

"I know," Anna said, but her eyes strayed often to the path through the trees.

Two days later Mijnheer De Jong returned, leading a small cow by a rope. Tied to the horse's sides hung two crates. Squawkings, scrabblings, and grunts came from them. Ma stood with her fist against her mouth, her eyes wide. Willem and Neil lifted down the crates and pried open the tops.

Anna squealed as a large rooster scrabbled his way out of the first crate, followed by three hens. The other crate revealed two large pigs with long necks and legs and a snout with tusks.

"They look like wild pigs," Pieter said.

Mijnheer De Jong laughed. "No," he said, "but you might not be able to keep them penned. If they get loose, let them run until you need some fresh meat. You'll never catch them, so you'll have to shoot them." He closed the crate. "Good thing you've got such a good marksman," he added, winking at Neil.

"I'll catch them when we need them," Neil said, throwing his shoulders back.

Pa tapped one of the crates with his foot. "How much do we owe you?" he said, a worry line creasing his forehead.

"Not a thing." Anna's father picked up the crate with the hogs and placed it in the shanty.

"Eggs," Ma said, her eyes shining. "And milk for the children." She shook her head. "We can't take such gifts," she began.

Mijnheer De Jong held up his hand. "We'll talk later," he said, glancing at Anna. Anna shoved her hands in the pockets of her apron and turned away. Pieter knew what the gifts meant. Anna and her father would leave soon.

Two more weeks went by. Anna's father made more trips, first to Allegan, then to Kalamazoo. Pieter began to hope he was buying supplies and bringing them to his acreage so he and Anna could set up housekeeping.

On the evening after Mijnheer De Jong came back from Kalamazoo, Pieter and Anna returned to the cabin from feeding the chickens to find the adults talking seriously.

Elizabeth looked up from the bench next to the fireplace and put her finger to her lips. She patted the seat next to her. Pieter and Anna slid onto the bench.

Pa leaned toward Mijnheer De Jong, his voice low and angry. His brows were drawn together and the grooves at the sides of his mouth looked deeper than ever.

"You can't do this to her," Pieter heard him say. He felt Anna stiffen next to him, her hands clenched together in her lap. A shiver of dread crept up his spine.

"It's only for a couple of years. Until she's older and I'm rich enough to build a decent house for her. I'll send for her then." Mijnheer De Jong swung his long legs away from the table and stood up.

"Anna," he said, "I'm going to California." He held up his hand as Anna started to speak. "I want you to stay with the

Dekkers. Just until I find enough gold to build you a grand house. Then I'll send for you."

Pieter couldn't believe what he was hearing. Anna's father was leaving her?

"I don't want a grand house, Pa." The bench rocked as Anna jumped up and grabbed her father around the waist. "I want you to stay here. All we need is a cabin and enough to eat. Please, Pa. We don't need to be rich. We need to be together."

"We will be, Anna. Just not yet. One day you'll have fine clothes and carriages. You won't have to work so hard." He put his hands on Anna's shoulders and pushed her away to look into her eyes. "Won't that be wonderful?"

Anna shook her head. Pieter saw the tears begin to roll down her cheeks. A lump rose in his throat. How could Mijnheer De Jong leave Anna? His thoughts swirled. But if Anna's father left for California, then Anna could continue to live with them. He didn't know whether to be happy for himself or sad for Anna. He looked at Mijnheer De Jong who was still smiling at Anna.

"You know I love you," Mijnheer De Jong said. "I'd take you with me if I could, but California's very rough. No place for young girls. I promise I'll send for you when you're older. Or maybe I'll come back here. We could build our house in Kalamazoo or Chicago." His eyes stared off into space as if he were seeing visions.

Anna reached up and shook him by the arms. "Please, Pa, stay here," she said. Her voice was clogged with tears. "I need a home now, not in a few years. Please." Her body began to shake as it had back on the ship after her mother's funeral.

"You have a home here. You have Mevrouw Dekker for a mother. You need a mother." Anna's father gathered her into his arms. "I've given Mijnheer Dekker some of the money I made selling the land. They'll be your family for a couple of years." He rocked Anna in his arms.

A burning anger rose in Pieter's chest. He stormed across

the room and out the door.

The night air closed cool and moist against his hot cheeks. He reached the edge of the clearing and dropped to the ground, staring up at the inky blackness of the night sky. The scent of pine needles rose in the air around him.

Thoughts chased themselves around in his head. Back and forth. Back and forth. How could Anna's father go off and leave her like that? He said he loved her. He hugged her constantly. His own pa would never leave his family. Through all the times Pieter had been angry at him for uprooting them, he had known that Pa would always be there.

He closed his eyes and saw Anna's father—laughing, talking, eyes sparkling, swinging Anna in his arms. Then he saw the face of his own pa—unsmiling, grim, set in lines of determination. He saw Mijnheer De Jong's blue eyes, shining with fun, loving, warm, restless, contrasted against Pa's gray eyes, cold, strong, unchanging, steady.

None of it made any sense. Pieter opened his eyes to find his cheeks wet with tears.

Chapter Twenty

Slowly things got back to normal after the day Anna's father rode away. Anna was quiet and solemn. Every chance they could, Pieter and Elizabeth spent time trying to cheer her up. Elizabeth taught her how to embroider yellow daisies on her apron.

Pieter gave her a picture he had drawn of her father. Anna cried when she saw it, but she hugged Pieter before pinning it to the wall on the girls' side of the loft.

When Anna received her first letter from her father, sent from Chicago on his way to California, she told Pieter, "You're my family now." Gradually, she began to smile again.

One morning at the breakfast table Pa said, "Pieter, do you think you and Anna might be able to find some nuts for us?"

Pieter jumped up. A day spent nutting instead of pulling weeds or chopping wood? "Of course we can," he said. "I saw some hickory trees the other day." Even his dislike of the forest couldn't dampen his excitement.

Anna turned from scraping grease from the skillet into a bowl. "If we could find some walnuts, Elizabeth and I could make cookies," she said.

"Walnuts might be hard to find, but there's a great stand of oaks up the stream a ways," Elizabeth added. "You could look there for acorns to roast this winter."

"Just don't get lost," Ma said. A worry line creased her forehead. "Stay close to the stream and within shouting distance of the cabin."

"Yes, Ma." Pieter reached for one of the baskets Elizabeth had woven during the quiet summer evenings. Anna grabbed another.

Ma handed Anna some cornbread. She tucked it into her

pocket while Pieter waited at the door, jiggling from foot to foot. If she didn't hurry, Pa might decide he needed them in the garden after all.

"Hurry, Anna," he said, pulling open the heavy wooden door of the cabin.

"Don't be so impatient." Anna slipped her feet into her wooden shoes, which were lined up with the others next to the door. In the house they went barefoot or wore only the heavy stockings Ma knitted for them.

Pieter ignored his shoes as he set off ahead of Anna across the clearing. He had learned to go barefoot outside, too, when he wasn't working with the ax. Pa made sure they wore their shoes around the heavy tree limbs and logs. Many a toe had been saved in the colony by the wooden shoes when an ax or hoe was swung awkwardly and hit someone on the foot.

One man in the area had tripped and fallen when a tree fell toward him, crashing onto his feet. When his fellow workers reached him, sure that his feet were crushed, the man crawled out from under the branches, leaving his shoes behind. The tree had fallen on the shoes, saving his feet from harm.

Pieter wriggled his toes in the dirt as he led the way under the trees along the Indian path. He knew the place with the oak trees that Elizabeth had mentioned.

"There are some plum trees along here too." He held back a branch for Anna so it wouldn't snap in her face.

"Ma would love some plums," Anna said, ducking under the branch.

Pieter's heart gave a little jerk. Anna had started to call his mother "Ma" after her father left. She still referred to her own mother as "Mama." He knew he shouldn't be jealous, but he felt a tiny spurt of anger every time he heard it.

She's not your ma, he wanted to say, but he clamped his lips together. After all, Anna had lost both her mother and father. He didn't want to hurt Anna, but he couldn't seem to control that nagging jealous voice at the back of his head.

He stomped up the trail ahead of Anna. *You're not a baby anymore,* he told himself. *Anna's only ten, she needs a mother to cuddle her. You're too big for that.* But he missed the attention he had received from Ma back in Zeeland. It was just one more change moving to this country had brought. He picked up a stick and banged it against every tree trunk he passed.

"Pieter, wait," Anna called, but he ignored her, letting the next tree branch snap back in her face. By the time he got to the grove of oaks, he was angry at himself for being so nasty as well as angry at Anna. He could hear her panting as she struggled to keep up.

"What's the matter with you?" Anna demanded when she finally reached him. Her eyes were dark with anger, her face red. She stamped her foot. "Why did you leave me behind like that?"

Pieter was speechless. He had seen Anna in tears many times—on the ship after her mother died and when her father left her. He had seen her tired and defeated. He had seen her happy while her father was still with them, but he had never seen her angry.

He dropped the fist full of acorns he had picked up and sat down on a large tree root. "I'm sorry," he mumbled.

Anna's eyes narrowed. "You should be," she said, shaking her basket at him. "Your legs are twice as long as mine. I'll tell Ma if you leave me behind again. What if I get lost?"

Pieter leaped up. It was too much. "She's not your ma. She's mine," he shouted. All the anger that had built up during the last week overflowed. "Just because your ma's dead, it doesn't mean you can have mine."

The minute the words were out of his mouth, Pieter wished them back. Anna's face turned as white as Ma's Sunday cap. Her body went rigid. For a long moment she stared at him, her mouth open, then her eyes widened in amazement.

"You're jealous," she said. "Of me." Her freckles stood out clearly in her white face. "You've got a mother and father who love you and take care of you, and you're jealous of me."

Pieter's body warmed from head to toe as a wave of shame swept over him. How could he have been so cruel to remind her that her father put more value on finding gold than he did on her? He opened his mouth to apologize, but Anna interrupted him.

"I thought you were the brother I never had," she said, her voice scornful. "And all along you were jealous."

"No, Anna," Pieter said. He wanted to tell her that she was like a sister, that she was part of the family, but the words stuck in his throat.

"You're nothing but a selfish beast. I don't need you to help me." Anna turned her back on him and stomped up the trail. "I'm going to find some plums for *Ma*," she called back, emphasizing the name as she disappeared beneath the trees.

Pieter rose to follow her, then stayed where he was. She was better off alone. Anna was right. He was selfish. His stomach twisted as he remembered that Pa had said the same thing when he ran off by himself to paint by the pond.

He picked up his basket and searched the ground for acorns. Why did Anna make him feel so jealous when Elizabeth didn't? *Because Elizabeth's just like Ma, always helping me and mothering me,* he answered himself. With Anna he had to be the strong one, the big brother.

"Pieter!" He heard Anna's screech from farther into the woods. "Come quick!" He dropped his basket of acorns and dashed toward the sound of her voice, his heart pounding. What was wrong? Had Anna seen a bear?

When he reached her, Anna was dancing from foot to foot beneath a plum tree, waving her arms at him.

"Bees!" she shouted. "Pieter, if we follow them, we could get some honey." She turned and darted off into the woods.

"No, Anna!" Pieter's heart thumped. "You'll get lost." Anna was already moving out of his sight. Scuffling his feet as much as possible to mark a path back to the stream, he followed her.

"Hurry, Pieter. I'm losing them," Anna called. Pieter stumbled over a root, righted himself, and looked back the way he had come. He could still see the clearing where the plum trees grew. Quickly he pulled a dead branch from the ground and stuck it upright in the tree roots as a marker.

Anna's voice was getting fainter. Fear gripped his heart. He couldn't let Anna get lost. He shouted again and began to run, slipping on the pine needles. The next time he looked he could no longer see the stream or the plum trees, but he knew which direction to follow back as long as the sun was out to give him a sense of direction.

He could still hear Anna shouting as he ran. He caught a glimpse of movement up ahead, heard a piercing shriek, and then nothing but silence.

"Anna!" Pieter shouted. His breath came in tiny gasps, his knees threatened to buckle under him. Where was she? Why didn't she answer?

He tripped and fell full length on the ground. He lay where he was, listening to the silence around him, straining to hear Anna's voice. Above him, a crow screeched angrily, then he thought he heard a groan.

He spit leaves out of his mouth and sat up. The groan came again, and he got up quietly, following the sound until he came to what looked like a huge pile of brush.

Anna lay in the middle of the pile. Her eyes were closed and her cap was twisted over one ear. Only the top half of her body showed. The rest of her had disappeared beneath the branches of the brush pile. She didn't move or answer Pieter's frantic call.

Chapter Twenty-One

"Anna." Pieter was about to clamber up the pile to her, then stopped and moved forward cautiously. It wouldn't help Anna if he fell too.

Anna groaned again, but her eyes remained closed. Pieter's chest tightened as he studied the situation. Two trees had fallen one across the other, forming a V. Branches and leaves had caught in the crook between the trees, and bushes and vines had grown up around them. In her eagerness not to lose sight of the bees, Anna had tried to climb over the fallen trees, not realizing how unstable the pile of brush was.

Pieter tested one of the huge logs carefully, found it unmovable, and climbed slowly toward Anna. He stretched his body along the trunk and patted her cheek gently, not wanting to startle her.

Anna's eyelids fluttered and opened. Her blue eyes looked dazed as they tried to focus on Pieter's face.

"What happened? Where . . ." Her words ended in a cry of pain as she tried to move.

"Lie still," Pieter said. "Where does it hurt?"

"My head," Anna answered. She moved her arms slowly, then drew in her breath sharply. "And my foot's caught. It hurts something awful."

"Don't move it. I'll see if I can get it loose." Pieter slid backward off the fallen log, then lay on his stomach to see if he could wriggle under the tree trunks.

"Be careful," Anna warned. "Don't let the logs fall on you."

"They're quite stable." Pieter pushed leaves and twigs out of his way as he crawled on his stomach until he could see

Anna's trapped foot. Her shoe had fallen off and her ankle was caught between two heavy tree limbs.

"It's not so bad," he called to her. "If we can move your foot backwards, you'll be free." He pulled several small branches away as Anna whimpered in pain. "Easy, now." Pieter took hold of Anna's foot and pulled it back as gently as he could.

Anna let out a howl and then her foot was free. Pieter grabbed her shoe and pushed himself backward from beneath the logs.

Tears streamed down Anna's cheeks as Pieter pulled her under the arms, and she struggled out of the pile of brush, dragging her injured foot.

"Are you all right?" Pieter asked as they sat on the pine needles, panting. Anna rubbed her twisted ankle, then wiggled her toes.

"I don't think it's broken," she said. "Help me up."

Pieter took her arm and pulled her up on one foot, but when she tried to take a step, she let out a cry of pain and sank down again.

"I don't think I can walk," she said. "You'll have to go for help."

Pieter shook his head. "I can't leave you here alone. You'll have to try to walk. Maybe I can make you a crutch." His voice trembled. It would take a long time for Anna to hobble back, but he knew he couldn't leave her. There were bears in the woods—and who knew what else.

As they stared at each other in dismay, the memory of their quarrel came flooding back. How could he ever have been so cruel to her, Pieter wondered.

"I'm sorry," he muttered, then felt his cheeks flush. Would Anna know what he was talking about?

"It's not your fault." Anna looked at the ground. "I was jealous too."

"You were? Of what?" Pieter tried to see her face, but Anna wouldn't look at him.

"Of you, silly. What do you think? You had a ma and pa

who loved you, a sister and brothers." Finally she looked up at him. "And you didn't even appreciate them," she said, drawing her eyebrows together in a scowl.

"I do too appreciate them." Pieter looked away from Anna's angry eyes. He picked up a large branch and began pulling leaves from it. He would make a crutch and they could get out of there.

"No, you don't," Anna challenged. "If I had parents like yours, I'd do anything they wanted me to, to show how much they mean to me."

Pieter pulled the last twig off the branch and sighed. "I was so jealous of your pa," he said. "He was just the kind of father I always wanted. My pa doesn't pay any attention to me unless it's to scold." He put the twig in his mouth and chewed on it, staring over Anna's head into the forest.

"He might if you'd let him. I see him looking at you when you don't know," Anna said. Pieter looked at her in surprise as she picked up her shoe and tried to put it on her foot, wincing from the pain.

"Yes, my father paid lots of attention to me and I love him," she added, "but he never took very good care of Mama and me. Why do you think Mama was already sick when we got on the ship at Rotterdam?" She picked up a handful of pine needles and let them sift through her fingers. "It was because Pa didn't leave us enough money for good food or a decent room when he left. He was always looking for a better life like your pa, but he never took care of the one he had."

She lifted her chin and her blue eyes met Pieter's with a clear look. "Mama had to work for other people to get the money for us to join Pa, and it wore her out," she said.

"I didn't know that." Pieter poked the stick through the leaves, disturbing a beetle from its sleep. "You never complained." He blushed to remember all the times he had grumbled and complained when asked to help.

"That's why I like your family so much. You all take care of each other and love each other, even if you don't show it much." She giggled suddenly. "In fact, you're just like your pa, all stiff and prickly like a porcupine most of the time."

"I am not!" Pieter pushed himself to his feet with the crutch.

"Are, too. You should see yourself. You look just like him. Without the beard." Anna doubled over with laughter.

Pieter opened his mouth to argue, then couldn't help laughing instead. "You don't look so good yourself," he said.

Leaves covered Anna's long skirt, twigs stuck out of her hair, and one ear peeked from under her cap that sat sideways on her head. "If I'm like my pa, then you have to listen to me," he added. "Let's eat the bread Ma gave us and then go home."

Anna nodded and pulled the cornbread out of one pocket and some small plums out of the other. Pieter picked the dirt off the squashed bread and looked at the sky through the trees. Low gray clouds covered the sun and it was difficult to tell how late it was.

"It must be afternoon," Anna said, noticing his anxious look. Plum juice dribbled down her chin. "We have plenty of time to get home before anyone begins to worry."

"I guess so," Pieter said. He had been searching the surrounding woods while they ate, not sure where he had exited when he first found Anna. He looked back at the sky. If the sun had stayed out, he could at least tell which direction to go to get back to the stream. Now he wasn't so sure.

He swallowed the last bite of plum and threw away the pit. He helped Anna to her feet, steadying her on one side while she used the crutch on the other. Moving slowly away from the fallen logs, they looked for signs of where they had run through the trees.

"It's all my fault." Anna tried to laugh. "If I hadn't followed the bees, we'd have our baskets full of nuts and be home by now. And we didn't even get any honey."

Pieter was tempted to agree with her. Anna's greediness for honey had landed them in this predicament, but he kept his mouth shut. There had been plenty of times he had complained about eating porridge without sweetener or bread with only butter on it.

"We'll find the way," he said with more confidence than he felt. He looked back through the trees at the pile of brush they had just left. "We'd better go back and try again. This isn't the right way, I'm sure."

The woods were darkening about them when they finally gave up and admitted that they were lost. In all their slow movement through the forest, they hadn't seen one of the markers Pieter had left as he followed Anna after the bees.

Anna sank down beneath a tree, her lips white with pain. "I can't go any farther," she said. "I'm only slowing you up. You could go faster without me." She pulled two plums out of her pocket and gave one to Pieter. "I'll wait right here and rest while you find someone to help us."

Pieter shook his head. "Even if I did manage to get home, how would I ever lead anyone back to you? None of my markers helped the first time, and it will be dark soon. Besides, I would never leave you here alone." His palms were sticky with perspiration and plum juice. His head ached from searching for signs of a path and listening for the trickling water of the creek.

"They'll be out looking for us by now," Anna said. She leaned back against the tree and smiled at him encouragingly. "Someone will find us."

Once again, Pieter found himself admiring her courage as he had on the ship and the canalboat. Their quarrel was forgotten. Their jealousy of each other seemed silly now. They might have to spend the night under these horrible trees, and Pieter was glad he wasn't alone.

"We could try calling. If someone's out looking, they might hear us," he suggested.

Anna nodded. "If we shout together we'll make more noise."

They shouted until they were hoarse, listening anxiously

between calls for any answering yell. Birds flew up from the trees, squawking wildly every time they raised their voices, and squirrels scolded from the branches above, but no human voices broke the otherwise silent forest. All around them the light faded until it seemed only the shadows remained.

All Pieter's old fear of the forest returned. The trees that had dropped nuts for them and sheltered them from the sun's hot rays were once again his old enemy, squeezing his heart of all feeling except fear. He clenched his hands together and took a deep breath, then another.

I can't let fear get the better of me this time, he thought. *I have Anna to think about, not just myself.* He closed his eyes tightly. What would Pa do in this situation?

A picture of Pa popped into his head, reciting a psalm as the flatboat moved through the rough waters of Lake Michigan on its way to Black Lake and the Holland Colony. What psalm had it been? The ninety-first, he thought. It had been like a prayer.

He couldn't remember the whole thing, only bits and pieces. He knew the first line. "'He who dwells in the shelter of the Most High will rest in the shadow of the Almighty.'" He felt a small hand slide into his and opened his eyes to see Anna nodding at him. He hadn't realized he had spoken aloud.

"'I will say of the Lord, 'He is my refuge and my fortress, my God, in whom I trust,'" Anna said. "I don't remember any more." She shivered, and for the first time Pieter remembered that the nights were much cooler now that summer was almost over. Besides sitting in the dark, they would be cold. Anna was still in pain. Pieter could tell by the small, tight sound of her voice.

The light was almost gone. "You will not fear the terror of the night,'" he said loudly, making Anna jump. "That's another verse."

Something crackled in the woods off to their right and Anna's hand tightened. Pieter raised his voice. "And there's another verse about commanding His angels to guard us and lift us up in their hands," he said.

The rustling was getting louder. It was an animal of some kind, Pieter was sure of it, but he couldn't see it in the darkness.

"'Because he loves me,' says the Lord, 'I will rescue him,'" Anna shouted suddenly.

"Hush." Pieter clamped his hand over her mouth, but it was too late. They heard panting, the bushes parted, and a large shadow moved slowly toward them. It stopped about ten feet away.

Every muscle in Pieter's body froze, and beside him Anna gave a small whimper. In front of them stood the huge gray bulk of a wolf. Its lips were drawn back over its teeth, and a low growl came from deep in its throat.

Chapter Twenty-Two

"Don't move," Pieter whispered as Anna stiffened beside him. They sat as still as they could, never taking their eyes from the wolf, who stared back at them without blinking. Slowly its growling stopped, and its lips settled back to normal. It didn't look so frightening once its teeth no longer showed, but neither of them stirred.

Then the wolf lowered its haunches and sat down. Its tail began to move slightly from side to side.

Pieter let out his breath in a long sigh. "I don't think it's a wolf," he whispered, barely moving his lips. "I think it's a dog."

"I've never seen a dog that looked like that," Anna whispered back.

"Neither have I, but there's something about it that acts more like a dog than a wolf." Pieter moved his hand a fraction of an inch to see if the wolf would react. When it didn't, he stretched out his hand toward it.

"I had a dog once," he said, still whispering. "His name was Sep. He sat just like that and only twitched his tail if he didn't know someone well. He's trying to decide if we're friends or not."

"Don't, Pieter," Anna whispered as the animal suddenly rose to all four feet as Pieter extended his hand. She smothered a scream with both hands as the huge beast moved toward them.

"It's all right, boy. Don't be afraid," Pieter said to it softly. He leaned forward. "Look, Anna, I'm sure it's wagging its tail." He could see the leaves move as the tail swished from side to side.

"I think it's a wolfhound," he said, daring to talk louder

now. "I heard about them. This one doesn't look like it's familiar with people. Maybe it belongs to someone who's looking for us." He sat up suddenly to shout for help, startling the big animal. It growled and bared its teeth again.

Anna grabbed his arm and pulled him back. "Wait and see," she said. "We can yell if it goes away again." They sat staring at the wolf-dog as it settled down in front of them, this time lying down completely, its massive head on its great paws.

"It looks like it's guarding us, like the angel in the psalm," Anna said. "I think you're right, Pieter. It is a dog. But who does it belong to?"

"Do you have any cornbread left?" Pieter held out his hand and Anna emptied her pocket of crumbs. "Let's see if it's hungry."

Once again he moved slowly toward the dog, holding out the crumbs in his hand. "Good dog," he said. "That's a good dog." The animal didn't move until Pieter was within a yard of it, then it sat up and stretched its nose to sniff at his hand.

"It is a dog, Anna. Look at it wag its tail." He reached up cautiously to pet the huge head. "Don't be afraid. Come and pet it."

Anna crawled across the space between them. The dog sniffed at her hand, then licked her cheek. Anna giggled. "That tickles," she said. She stroked the dog's neck. "I've never had a dog. I didn't know they were so soft."

"Bram!" The call startled all three of them. The dog's ears went up and its head swiveled in the direction of the sound. Then, with a tremendous bark, which was half howl, it was gone as quickly as it had come.

"No! Wait!" Anna yelled. "Oh, Pieter, don't let it go. It was guarding us, I know it. It came because we prayed for help." She tried to stand and toppled over as her weak ankle buckled under her.

Pieter began to shout, and Anna joined in. "Help! We're lost. Help, please!" he shouted, then shushed Anna to see if he could hear anything. Off in the distance the dog barked again. An owl hooted above their heads. They shouted again, then strained to hear. Was the barking coming closer?

"He's coming back," Pieter said as Anna clapped her hands. "Here, we're over here," he called.

The barks were getting louder. "He's bringing someone," Anna said. "Hurrah! We're found." She pushed her cap, which had fallen sideways again, straight on her head.

Then the dog was back, wagging its tail and licking their faces. Anna threw her arms around it.

Pieter looked up to see the dog's owner. A man was standing back in the shadows beneath the trees. Pieter could see a tall figure, covered in deerskin. Even his head was covered with a large buckskin hat with a wide brim that left his face in shadow. As the man moved forward, Pieter saw a bushy, sandy-colored beard and shaggy hair that fell into his eyes. Under his arm he carried a rifle.

"Sit, Bram," the man said. "What have we here?" he added, stopping a few feet from them and shaking his head. His voice sounded rusty, as if he rarely used it.

"Is it an Indian?" Anna whispered in Pieter's ear, her fingernails digging into his arm.

Pieter smothered a laugh. "Not with that beard and speaking our language," he said, trying to see the man's face clearly. Was he truly a Hollander? He certainly didn't look like one. Even his boots were made of deer hide.

"Who are you?" the man asked. He moved forward, towering over them until he bent to pat Bram's head as if to keep his eyes hidden from them.

"I'm Pieter Dekker and this is my sister Anna De Jong." The words were out before he realized what he had said, but he saw Anna's eyes widen with pleasure. *My sister*, he thought. It suddenly seemed the most natural thing in the world to call her that.

"We were picking nuts and I chased some bees and my foot got caught and I hurt my ankle and Pieter pulled me out and then we got lost," Anna said, all in a rush.

Pieter saw the stranger's teeth gleam as his lips turned up in a smile. He strained to see the man's eyes, but the shadow of the buckskin hat hid them. He realized that the man hadn't been part of a search party looking for them or he would have known who they were.

"Who are you?" Pieter asked boldly, since the man didn't seem willing to introduce himself. "Where do you live?"

The man waved vaguely toward the forest. "Can you walk?" he asked Anna, ignoring Pieter's questions. When she shook her head, he handed Pieter his gun, scooped Anna up in his arms, and jerked his head at Pieter. "Come," he said.

Anna chattered happily to her rescuer as they strode along. Above them the clouds parted and pale moonlight filtered down through the leaves, giving the woods a ghostly quality. Only Bram seemed real as he bounded back and forth just as Sep used to do.

"Where are we going?" he asked, trying to squelch his uneasy feelings. It was hard to keep up with the stranger's strides while carrying the rifle. He was about to call out when the man ahead stopped. Pieter ran to catch up and found Anna and the man standing in front of a small clearing.

"Welcome to my home," the man said. "We'll stop for a bite of food, then get you back." He led the way toward a small structure set back in the trees.

"Adrian knows where we live," Anna said, peering over the stranger's shoulder at Pieter. "He can find anything, even in the dark." She seemed to have made friends with the man while they walked.

Pieter followed them up the path. A small yard had been cleared in front of a tiny hut made of intertwined branches and twigs. As they moved toward the door of the hut, Anna let out a terrified squeal and pointed to a gigantic shadow that loomed just at the edge of the clearing. "A bear," she cried. Pieter dropped the gun and turned to run.

Laughter rumbled up from the man in the buckskin.

"Don't be afraid," he said. "Come and look." He led them toward the unmoving figure as Bram barked at it and jumped up, putting his paws on the back of the giant bear.

Pieter drew in his breath in a hiss of delight as he realized what stood in front of him. The bear had been carved from the trunk of a tree, each detail so intricately cut that he could see the individual hairs of the shaggy coat in the moonlight.

"Put me down. I want to touch it." Anna squirmed suddenly. The man set her on her feet as she ran her hand over the nose of the huge bear. "It's beautiful," she said, turning to their rescuer, her eyes shining. Then she pointed behind Pieter. "Look, Pieter. There and there."

Pieter felt the weight of the day's problems lift from his shoulders as he looked about him. Standing all around the edges of the small yard were animals. A doe bent to touch her fawn with her nose. A fox with a bushy tail looked ready to dart back into the woods at any moment. Squirrels perched on tree stumps, cracking nuts, and a wild turkey fluffed its feathers next to three fat geese. A wolf guarded the door with a ferocious snarl on its face, much worse than any they had seen on Bram.

To Pieter's eyes they looked more beautiful than real animals. The artist had captured the freedom of each creature and frozen it in time so they could see the wild nature that lived within. If only he could make paintings someday that came even halfway close to the beauty he saw before him, he would be satisfied.

"Did you do these?" he asked, breathless with delight.

The woodsman's smile sparkled in the shaggy beard. "No one else lives here," the man said. He picked up the gun Pieter had dropped. "Come in. We shouldn't delay any longer. Your folks are probably sick with worry."

Pieter helped Anna into the hut as the man lit a lantern in the middle of his table and bent to stir up the fire. As the soft glow filled the tiny room Pieter laughed aloud. Parading

across the room was a mother skunk followed by four wad-
dling babies. A porcupine, each quill clearly outlined, slept in
a corner, and a raccoon sat on its haunches nibbling on a bit
of fish held daintily between its paws.

On the table a duck's head rose from a large chunk of
wood. Carving knives littered the table, which was covered
with wood shavings. The carved figures seemed to move as
the firelight flickered over them.

Anna settled herself in a low tree-stump chair. The man in
the deerskin turned from stirring the fire. He took off his hat,
and for the first time Pieter could see his face clearly in the
light from the lamp. Brilliant green eyes sat deep in a bronzed
face. The man had pushed his straggly hair behind his ears,
exposing his face, as if he no longer feared them seeing him.

"My name is Adrian Vreeke," he said in his gruff voice. "I'm
sorry I didn't introduce myself earlier. I don't always like people knowing who I am." The green eyes darkened.

Pieter said nothing, but Anna reached out and touched
him lightly on the hand. "We won't tell anyone where you
live, if you'd rather be alone," she said. A giggle escaped her
lips. "We couldn't tell anyway. We have no idea where we are."

Adrian's mouth broadened in a wide smile as he looked at
Anna's laughing face. "I don't think I mind the two of you
knowing about me," he said.

Pieter smiled back at him. "You can trust us," he said,
stroking Bram's shaggy coat as he sat with his head on
Pieter's knee, just like Sep once did. "But why do you live
alone in the woods?"

Adrian turned to stare into the fire for so long, Pieter
thought he had gone too far in being so curious.

"I haven't always been alone," he said finally in a low
voice. "I came to the Holland Colony in the spring of '47 with
my wife and little girl." He poked at the fire with his stick.
"She was six years old. She looked a lot like you." He raised
his eyes briefly to Anna. "Same curly hair that wouldn't stay

under her cap. Same dimple in her cheek when she laughed." Dark shadows flickered in his eyes.

"What happened?" Anna whispered.

"It was a terrible year in the colony," Adrian said. "We lived in huts worse than this one." His gaze swept over the tiny room. "Some people had nothing but tents made from old bedsheets or quilts. It rained all the time. There wasn't enough food."

He got up abruptly, took a loaf of bread from a shelf, and began cutting thick slices. Pieter and Anna sat as still as the carved figures around them.

"People began to get sick," he continued. "Every hut or tent or cabin was filled with sickness. There were no doctors and no medicine." He set down the knife and stared into a corner of the hut. "More and more immigrants kept coming. There was no place to put everyone and no food to feed them. Most were very poor. And then they began dying."

Silence settled over the cabin. Pieter knew from Willem that the past year had been hard, but Willem didn't like to talk about it and had never told them many details. For the first time the hardships became real to him. He could see the people shivering from fever under thin blankets in the makeshift huts. He felt the hunger that twisted their insides.

The fire crackled and sputtered. Adrian pulled a tin cup from the shelf and filled it with water from a barrel near the door.

"My wife got sick first," he said. "For three days I prayed for her to get better. Then my little Janna caught the fever." His voice rasped, and he cleared his throat. "I caught it the day my wife died. I couldn't even see her buried. Two weeks later, when I recovered, my Janna was gone too." He sat down at the table and lowered his head into his hands. Anna got up and limped to his side. She laid her hand on his head.

"I was so angry at God. I didn't understand why He had brought us here to die. I left the colony as soon as I could." Adrian's voice was muffled. "I've been here ever since. Just me, my carving, and God."

He raised his head and looked about him at the wooden animals. "I thought I'd left God behind, but He wouldn't leave me alone. I worked out my anger through recreating His beauty around me. I know struggle and sorrow are as much a part of life as laughter and joy," he said, "and always will be. But it's hard to accept when it happens to you."

Tears glistened in his eyes as he looked at Anna. "The Bible never promises a life without troubles, only that God will be there in the pain with us." He blinked away his tears and smiled at them. "You're the first people I've really talked to since I left the colony. I've been thinking of going back to visit some old friends, but it's been so long I felt awkward about it. Now that I have new friends, maybe it will be easier."

"Oh, yes," Anna said. "You can meet Ma and Pieter's pa, and everyone. And we can come visit you and Bram."

"If that's all right with you," Pieter added quickly. Anna's enthusiasm was overwhelming. He didn't want to invade Adrian's privacy, but he wanted to come back and see the animals in daylight. Maybe Adrian would teach him how to carve. He could make a figure of Sep from the drawings he had.

As if she had read his thoughts, Anna said, "Pieter's an artist too. He draws great pictures. He drew one of my pa that looks just like him."

Adrian smiled at Pieter, then raised an eyebrow at them and said, "I wondered why you two had different names when you said you were brother and sister. You know, then, what it's like to lose someone you love."

"Only Anna," Pieter said. He explained how Anna had come into the family.

"Someday your father will come back," Adrian said, taking Anna's chin in his hand when Pieter finished. "He couldn't possibly stay away from such a daughter for long. In the meantime, you have two more fathers. Pieter's pa and now me. Or if that's too many, I'll be another brother. Now, finish your bread and we'll be on our way."

It was nearly midnight when they reached the clearing near the stream where Anna had been picking plums before running off to chase the bees. Anna was sound asleep on Adrian's shoulder. Pieter trudged behind them like a sleepwalker. Up ahead, Bram began to bark, and Pieter heard a familiar voice calling. He shouted back, and a few minutes later, Willem burst from the trees around them, his face anxious and strained.

"Pieter!" Willem set down his lantern and grabbed Pieter under the arms, swinging him up in a bear hug. "Thank God! Where have you been? We've been looking for hours."

Anna woke up and blinked sleepily in the light from Willem's lantern. "Are we still found?" she asked. Adrian laughed and set her on her feet. She leaned against him as Willem squatted down to hug her.

"Yes, you're found," he said, looking up curiously at Adrian. "Now let's get to the cabin quickly. Ma is terrified. Pa and Neil are still in the woods searching for you."

"Go find them and bring them back, Bram," Adrian ordered. Bram set off with a ferocious barking into the woods. "He'll find them." Adrian shyly held out his hand to Willem and introduced himself.

"Thank you, thank you for finding them," Willem said. "Come back to the cabin." Pieter could see that Willem was bursting with curiosity about Adrian, but Adrian pulled back. "I'd best be getting home," he said.

"No," Anna wailed. "You promised. You said you'd be friends. Ma will want to thank you." She grabbed Adrian's hand and began to pull him up the path.

As Adrian followed them, Pieter ran ahead, shouting. He knew the way now. Before he got to the cabin, the door was flung open, and he saw Ma in the doorway. He threw himself at her like a little boy. As Ma's arms closed around him, he thought how good it was not to have to be the big brother all the time.

He was glad he wasn't Pa, responsible for all of them every day.

Then the little cabin filled with people. Ma couldn't stop crying. Even Elizabeth hugged Adrian, who looked extremely uncomfortable with all the attention heaped on him. They heard Bram's tremendous bark, and then Pa and Neil were there, and the hugging started all over again.

When all the commotion died down, Pieter found himself on the bench next to Pa, Pa's arm around him. Anna sat on Ma's lap. Adrian had taken a chair in the darkest corner of the room, letting Anna and Pieter tell the story of their long day.

Pieter knew they were all curious about Adrian, but he and Anna kept his story to themselves. Adrian could tell the rest of them after he came to know them better.

Pieter knew they would always remain friends. Now that they had found each other, none of them would ever be the same. Adrian had someone to remind him of his little girl. Anna had someone who knew what it was like to lose the people you loved most in the world. He had found a friend to share his love of creating things that reflected the beauty around them. *And a dog,* he thought, looking down as Bram slapped his heavy tail against the floor, his head on Pieter's foot.

"And now we have a new neighbor we can go visit, and who can come for dinner," Anna finished, echoing Pieter's thoughts. "If we can ever find his house again."

Adrian's laughter rumbled from the corner where he sat. "I'll make sure you can find it," he said. "Perhaps Neil and I could hack out a path and blaze a trail through the trees."

"Until then, you'll have to come to visit us," Pa said, getting to his feet. "I don't want my children getting lost again." He put his hand on Pieter's head. "Although I'm proud of them for the way they stuck together and helped each other out."

Anna giggled and Pieter blushed to think how they had quarreled. That part of the story was just between the two of them. *After all,* Pieter thought, *that's what brothers and sisters do.*

Chapter Twenty-Three

One fall morning toward the end of September, Pieter woke to a smell he hadn't experienced since leaving Zeeland. He bounded out of bed and clattered down the ladder still in his nightclothes.

"I smell pancakes!" he shouted. "Ma, how'd you do it?"

"The hens." Elizabeth's eyes sparkled. "They laid their first eggs. After all, it is a special day."

A special day? Pieter glanced down the table at the row of laughing faces. He remembered he was still in his night-clothes and scrambled back up the ladder to dress.

What was going on? Why hadn't he heard the older boys getting up? Usually they made enough noise to wake the cow. It was still early, the sun barely lighting the sky behind the trees. He pulled on his pants and shirt and hurried back down the ladder.

"Surprise!" Shouts and laughter greeted him. Anna bounced up and down in her chair. Neil banged his spoon against the bottom of a pan. Willem grinned broadly. The table was set with a special blue napkin at Pieter's place.

"Don't you know what day it is, Pieter?" Elizabeth asked, clapping her hands.

"I do believe he's lost track of the days completely," Ma said. She turned from the oven that was built into the side of the fireplace, a steaming stack of pancakes piled on a plate. "It's your birthday, Pieter. Happy twelfth birthday."

Hands pulled at Pieter. Congratulations swarmed around him. His back was slapped. Finally, he settled into his chair in a daze. He reached for his fork and his hand froze. Next to his plate rested his drawing book and charcoal pencils. He looked at Pa, his cheeks warm.

"Happy birthday, Pieter," Pa said.

"Is it really my birthday?" Pieter asked. "I completely forgot. I really did."

"I know," Pa said with a half smile on his face. "Imagine, Pieter forgetting his own birthday."

As the laughter swirled around him, Pieter wondered how he could have forgotten. Just last March he had thought about nothing but his school, his teacher, his artwork, his dog, his friends. Now he'd been so busy, he'd forgotten his own birthday.

"Eat, Pieter," Pa broke into his reverie.

The pancakes vanished quickly. When Pieter finished his milk, Pa said, "And now the birthday surprise. We have a lot of work to do today and tomorrow, but we all agreed to give you Saturday as a day free from work. You may do whatever you want."

"You can sleep all day," Ma said, "or fish or swim in the pond."

"Or read or draw," added Elizabeth. "Anna and I will do all your chores."

A whole day with no work to do. Just what he had wished for when he read Dirk's letter. He thought he would do all the things he hadn't had time for all summer. Then he remembered one special thing that no one had had time for, not even Willem.

That night he sneaked a look at Willem's letter that was lying on the shelf where he had placed it so long ago. He memorized the section number and coordinates for Willem's land.

Early Saturday morning, while the others were still sleeping, he climbed quietly down from the loft. He left a note, stuffed some bread and butter into his pockets, along with his pencils and book, and made his way down to the creek.

It was still dark, but the birds were waking. They chirped and fluttered in the treetops and brush, looking for their breakfast. The misty air was fresh and cool on his face as he followed Bark Creek west.

Often he had to push his way through thick bushes that

grew along the banks of the stream. Occasionally, the ground smoothed beneath his feet and he knew he had found an Indian trail. When the trails led back into the woods, he kept to the stream. He felt more comfortable with the forest around him now, but he remembered how quickly it had swallowed them up when he and Anna had gotten lost.

The sun rose, sparkling through the trees. As he pushed through the thick underbrush, a vision of Sep rose in his mind. He saw Sep and Dirk running straight across the flat land, unhindered by trees and bushes. Sep was barking joyously, chasing a rabbit. He was glad Sep had stayed in Zeeland.

A prickly vine grabbed at his pants leg and he stopped to untangle it. He sat at the edge of the stream to rest. The air about him brightened, shimmering gold and green as the mist faded. Birds called sweetly. The stream gurgled over the stones. High above his head the tall trees rustled, making soft music in the morning breezes.

I feel like I'm in church, Pieter thought, awed by the beauty surrounding him. *God made this beautiful land,* he thought. *Just like He made Zeeland in the Netherlands. God made this stream and the tiny flowers.* He remembered part of the psalm they had sung their first Sunday in church.

"Then all the trees of the forest will sing for joy; they will sing before the Lord . . ." Pieter murmured. Even these huge trees were part of God's Creation. He reached out to grab a small fish that glided by, but missed. He scrambled up and pushed on. At one point he jumped the stream in one long leap, then looked at his legs in surprise.

"I guess I've grown," he said aloud. He patted his stomach, tight and flat from the stooping and bending of chopping and dragging underbrush. He stretched his arms straight out, laughing at the way his wrists stuck out, the sleeves of his shirt too short.

He walked easily on bare feet. A chipmunk scampered across his path. Two squirrels crashed through the bushes in a game of chase. He knew there were deer about, maybe even a bear or large cat, but they kept to themselves.

The sun was about a quarter of the way up the sky when he saw a clearing off to the side. He left the stream and headed for it, excitement making his breath come quickly. At the edge he stopped, tiredness dropping from him. He had found Willem's land, he was sure. It was just as he had described it.

The clearing was small, surrounded by tall elms and birches, dotted with the stumps of felled trees. In the middle stood a tiny half-finished cabin. Tangled vines and small bushes already sprouted from the dirt floor inside. The stones of the chimney had tumbled and scattered like leaves on the ground.

But could he be sure? He moved toward the edge of the clearing, searching for the *blessen*, the ax marks that survey-ors left on trees at the corners of the lots. He had just decided he didn't dare get any farther from the clearing when he found the first one.

Yes! This was it, the section and lot numbers carved in the tree matched the ones in Willem's letter. Keeping as straight a line as he could, he turned west. His eyes on the trees, he searched for the northwest corner of the lot, then stopped, his heart knocking against his chestbone.

A faint swooshing sound came through the trees in front of him. Back and forth, back and forth, swish, swish. The sound of water. The sound waves made lapping against the shore.

Pieter began to run. He crashed through the trees and bushes, scratching his face and hands. A shirtsleeve caught on a branch and he heard it rip as he tore loose. The smell of fish wafted toward him. He plunged through a particularly dark stand of cedars, and there before him was the lake.

Chapter Twenty-Four

Lake Michigan. Pieter drew in deep breaths of tangy air and gazed out across the wide expanse. Far out on the horizon the water was green and smooth as glass. Closer in it reflected the blue of the sky, ruffling into tiny waves capped with white foam that swished onto the sand.

He slid down a sand hill, crossed the beach, and waded into the water, yelping at its coldness. Reaching down, he splashed the water high into the air, then turned to look back toward Willem's property.

As far as he could see to his right and left, rolling dunes stretched along the shore, topped by tall trees. Trees that no longer frightened him. He stretched his arms over his head lazily, then swung back to face the lake. Above his head gulls swooped. Above the gulls, fat, puffy clouds floated across the blue of the sky, just as they did back in Zeeland.

"Happy birthday, Pieter," he yelled. He stood gazing out at the lake until his legs were numb with cold, then turned and waded back to the beach.

The hours passed quickly. He didn't go back to Willem's clearing. He ate his bread and butter sitting on a log that had dropped from an overhanging tree, his feet in the water.

In the afternoon he paddled happily, finding glistening pebbles beneath the small waves that lapped against the shore. He searched the beach for shells, wondering what tiny creatures had made each one. He tasted a bit of seaweed floating beneath the surface, just to see what it was like.

The sun warmed his head and shoulders, the water cooled his feet. He breathed deeply of the moist, fishy air. When the sun got too hot, he found a shady spot at the edge of the forest and scooped out a hollow in the sand.

Pulling his drawing book from his pocket, he paged through it slowly. It was almost full of drawings now. The Zeeland countryside, Sep, Dirk, the Atlantic Ocean, the canalboat, their cabin in the middle of the clearing, the church in town. He added a picture of Adrian and Bram surrounded by Adrian's carved figures, then he began to draw the lake. He wished he had paints, but he did the best he could. His eyes closed and he fell asleep.

When he woke, the sun blazed halfway down the sky. He knew he'd better start back if he wanted to get home before dark, but he was reluctant to leave. Even the fear of being lost again couldn't make him hurry.

He rolled down his pants legs and crossed the sand slowly, searching for the opening in the dunes where the stream emptied into the lake. Bushes rustled beside him and he started as a tall figure emerged from the forest.

Pa! What was he doing here?

Pa stood for a long time, his hands in his pockets, not looking at Pieter. Instead, he gazed out across the lake. Pieter knew that Pa was remembering Zeeland, with its many inlets and waterways. Then Pa did a strange thing. He took his hands out of his pockets and stretched his arms out toward the lake, just as Pieter had done.

Pa dropped his arms and crossed the sand to Pieter. Still he didn't speak. He kicked off his shoes, rolled up his pants legs, and waded into the water. Pieter followed him to the edge.

"Your ma was worried about you," Pa said without turning around. "She was afraid you'd get lost again."

Pieter didn't answer. Pa swung around to look back at the forest, then out at the lake again. Finally he looked directly at Pieter.

"But I wasn't worried," he said. "I knew you'd be all right. I knew you'd stick to the stream this time." He reached into the water and picked up a pebble, turning it over in his big hands.

"You found Willem's property," he said. He waded out of the water and lowered himself to the sand. "We're probably not more than two or three miles from home." He patted the sand next to him. "Sit down, Pieter."

Pieter plopped himself down next to Pa. A gull screeched above them. The sun sent long fingers of red across the clouds.

Pa reached inside his shirt and pulled out a rolled piece of paper. He handed it to Pieter. "This belongs to you," he said.

Pieter took the paper and unrolled it. It was his painting, the one he thought he'd lost. The Zeeland countryside was as green as the day he had painted it. The windmill rose tall above the water, and Sep raced along under the clear blue sky. A lump rose in his throat.

"I went back to get your painting that afternoon," Pa said. "Work is important for our survival, but beauty is too. I'd forgotten that. As soon as winter comes and we have more time, I'll carve a frame for it. It will look good hanging over the mantelpiece." Pa brushed his hand across the painting. "When we get a little money for extras, we'll get you some real paints and you can paint us a bigger one. So we never forget our homeland."

Pieter's throat hurt. He nodded. No, he would never forget Zeeland.

"We'd best be getting back," Pa said, but he didn't move. Behind them a late afternoon breeze set the high branches of the trees rustling.

"Listen, Pa," Pieter said. "The trees are singing."

"Singing for you," Pa said. He put his hand on Pieter's shoulder and pushed himself to his feet. He held out his hand and Pieter took it, letting Pa pull him up. Pa smiled, a smile tinged with sadness.

"You're not a little boy anymore, are you?" he said. "You'll be up to my shoulder in no time. You were the one I was most afraid for. I wasn't sure you would survive the journey. You were always so sickly. Now look at you."

Pieter laughed. He had no idea what he looked like. He knew he was taller, stronger. He figured he must be as brown from the sun as the others. He hadn't known that Pa worried about him.

"I'm strong now," he said.

"Yes." Pa turned to look at the trees at the edge of Willem's lot. "Willem will need help clearing this land," he said. "He's a man now and will need a house of his own one of these days. Now that our cabin is finished, I think I can spare the two of you one day a week. The rest of us can pick the corn and dig the potatoes." Pa rubbed the side of his nose. "Do you think you'd like that?"

Pieter let out a whoop of joy. "You know I would," he shouted. He would be only too happy to be near the water, to smell the fish, to sleep on the beach. He would find a way to make more watercolors and paint the lake. *At sunrise,* he thought. *In the middle of the day, at sunset, and maybe even at night.*

"I'll build a boat," he said. "I'll catch fish and bring them home for supper. Maybe we can build a pier." He took a deep calming breath and grinned at Pa's stern look.

"Maybe next summer," Pa said. "First you help Willem."

"Yes, Pa," Pieter said. "And maybe I can go to school when they start one. When it's too cold to work on the land."

Pa nodded. "You're a good boy, Pieter," he said. He cleared his throat gruffly and bent to pick up his shoes. "Let's go home now."

"Yes," Pieter agreed. "Let's go home." He followed Pa up the beach to the stream. He took one last look at the lake, then turned and stepped after Pa into the darkness beneath the trees.

From *The Journey of Hannah…*

"Is that you, Hannah?" Mistress Weston called.

"Yes, ma'am," Hannah answered, coming to the door of the public room, where she saw three men dressed in buckskin sitting at a table. They each had one of the heavy tavern mugs in front of them, and one of them shuffled a deck of cards through his fingers.

"We have guests for the evening," the mistress said. "Let's see what a good meal we can set before them." She smiled her leering smile and arched her eyebrows at Hannah.

Hannah pretended not to see. "I'll start supper," she said, turning to go back into the kitchen.

Soon the mistress followed. "A rich night for us, my girl!" she crowed, picking up a knife and slicing into a crusty loaf of bread. "They carry the wealth of a settlement, on their way to buy supplies in Virginia. Of course, we won't take it all— just enough to help us and not hurt them too badly!"

Mistress Weston's unpleasant laugh crawled down Hannah's spine, but she went on frying ham in the big iron skillet over the fire, wiping the sweat from her face with the hem of her apron.

The mistress put the bread in the oven to warm and set a fresh pot of coffee on the fire. "I'm so glad Weston brought us those chickens," she said. "Eggs cost us practically nothing now, except a little corn and some effort. I'll get some to go with that ham." Humming under her breath, she went to the storeroom.

It seemed to Hannah that they no sooner had taken the plates of food to the men than they were calling for more. But she hoped they would sit there eating, drinking, and playing cards all night. All too soon, though, she heard their footsteps mounting the stairs.

"You know what to do, girl," the mistress said, sticking her head in at the kitchen door on her way upstairs. "And I expect you to place more than six coins in my hand in the morning!"

"Mistress Weston," Hannah began, "please don't make me do this again! I will do anything you ask of me. Just don't make me do this!"

The mistress turned to stare at her, as though she couldn't believe what she had heard. Then her eyes narrowed. "You will do what I say, girl," she said between clenched teeth, "or I will see that Weston beats you within an inch of your life!"

Hannah swallowed hard. "Beat me, then, mistress, but don't make me do this!"

Suddenly the mistress smiled, a grim, thin-lipped smile. "All right, girl. You don't have to do it."

Hannah watched her warily. She supposed she should have been relieved, but she knew it wasn't going to be that easy.

"But your days next door with your precious Miss Rachel are over! Do you understand?" the mistress said with a mocking smile.

Hannah looked down at her feet, trying to hide her emotions. She knew that to let Mistress Weston know how badly her punishment hurt would only encourage more of the same.

"Yes, ma'am, I understand," she answered, meeting the woman's narrow gaze without flinching.

The mistress nodded, and apparently satisfied that she would be obeyed, went on upstairs.

Hannah sank down on the bench by the table and laid her head on her crossed forearms. She would have to wait until all were asleep before attempting to fulfill her assigned tasks.

"I can't do it!" she said aloud, raising her head. But how could she refuse? The promised beating was nothing compared to the threat that she could never go back to Miss Rachel's!

A loud snore from upstairs told her that at least one man was asleep. She glanced at the open window at the front of the kitchen. It was as black as the inside of a tunnel outside. Inside, the faint glow from the dying fire threw flickering shadows over the log walls. Out back, she could hear the lowing of the master's new cow, calling to the calf she had been forced to leave behind on the farm. But in here, except for the ticking of the clock on the public-room mantel and the snores upstairs, the tavern was wrapped in silence.

Were there more snores in the room above, now? She couldn't be sure all three men were asleep, but if she had to be a thief, she supposed she'd better be about it. She sighed and pushed herself up from the table.

As she placed one foot on the bottom riser of the stairs, the butterflies tumbled wildly in the pit of her stomach. Nausea rose in her throat. *How can I do this terrible thing again tonight and then face Miss Rachel the day after tomorrow?* she wondered. Yet, if she didn't obey the mistress, she knew she would never be with Miss Rachel again.

Either way, I lose Miss Rachel, she thought despairingly. *And she's the only good thing in my life!*

All at once, Hannah knew what she had to do. She turned from the stairs, went into the storeroom, and grabbed her other dress and the shawl Mistress Weston had given her in exchange for Mistress Annabelle's blue cloak. She carried them back into the kitchen, spread the shawl on the table, and rolled the dress up on top of it. Then she added a loaf of bread, a knife, and a tin mug.

She looked around, and her gaze fell on two left-over sweet potatoes in a wooden bowl. Quickly, she wrapped them in a small cloth and added them to her pile. Then she tied two corners of the shawl together and repeated the process with the other two corners.

She ran back to the storeroom, got her shoes, and though they were getting too tight, stuffed her feet into the soft leather. Even feet toughened from going summer bare would need protection from the rough traveling she must do.

Then Hannah dug in a crack in the crumbling chinking between the logs, and pulled out the two gold coins Master Alex had given her that day on the wharf at Charleston when he had left her to the mercy of the Westons. She carried the coins back into the kitchen, held them in her hand a moment, then laid one on the table to pay for what she had taken. The other, she tucked into her bundle.

What would Master Alex do if he knew how she was treated by the people to whom he had sold her? But even if she could find him, she knew he could do nothing to help her. She belonged to the Westons, and there was nothing she could do but obey them.

Or run away! she thought, slipping the back-door latch carefully out of its holding bar and pushing the door open wide enough to squeeze through. She eased the door shut behind her and leaned against it.

There was no moon, and only a few stars had braved the dark sky. She could barely see her hand before her. It was just another shape of darkness, like the outline of the stable to her left. Beyond it, the stone house was visible as a lighter shadow among shadows.

To her right, Miss Rachel's brick house had disappeared into a shroud of trees and darkness. She wished she could say good-bye, could tell Miss Rachel how much their time together had meant to her. But the less her friend knew about her disappearance, the better it would be for Miss Rachel if the Westons came to question her.

The darkness was like a thick cover around her. Would she be able to make her way through it to put enough distance between her and this place before daybreak, when her disappearance was sure to be discovered? How long did she have? It was well into the early morning hours, for she had heard the clock strike midnight some time ago.

Where should she go? The master had set bloodhounds on Bo's trail. She felt sure he would do the same with her. She had heard talk on Sunrise Island of how runaway slaves would wade in streams to destroy any scent the hounds might have followed. Here, though, there was only the river. She was a strong swimmer, but how could she get her bundle across without getting it wet?

If she went down to the riverbank, would there be a boat she could use to cross the river? But if she left it on the other side, wouldn't the handlers simply bring the dogs across and start them on her trail there?

She edged around the corner of the tavern and walked toward the street in front of it. Maybe she should just follow the road out of Frankfort and wade the first stream she found, hoping it would be soon enough to escape the relentless hounds.

Hannah took a deep breath, entered the street, and turned to her right. She strode rapidly down the dirt track, hoping there were no bumps or holes to trip her in the dark.

Suddenly, the moon came out, impaling her dark figure in the middle of the road, exposing her to any who might be watching. She edged over toward the trees at the side of the road, praying no one had seen.

For a time, she stumbled along inside the line of trees, then moved over to follow along the top of the riverbank. From the tree-lined cliffs, a screech owl gave his lonely call, and was answered from somewhere up-river. She glanced quickly at the opposite bank, where the eerie green glow of phosphorous, or wildfire, winked at her from under rocks and fallen logs. Or was it all wildfire? Were the eyes of wild animals watching her too?

She shuddered. Then under her breath she began to sing some of the Gullah songs they had sung at the Praise House back on Sunrise Island. It pushed the fear away, and enabled her to keep up a steady progress away from Frankfort.

By the time the sky began to lighten, her empty stomach had been grumbling for some time. She sat down on the roots of a huge sycamore tree, opened her bundle, tore off a chunk of bread and ate it hungrily. She wondered how far she had come.

It seemed that she had been walking forever! But she knew she couldn't be far enough away from the tavern to rest long. Soon she was off again, heading upstream. She had no idea where she was going, but she knew she had to keep traveling or be caught. Often, runaway slaves did not get a second chance!

As the sun's rays touched the water, she heard the hounds. Fear drove her over the riverbank and into the water. She slung her bundle over her shoulder and waded out into the water. Soon she felt the bottom slip away from under her feet. She began a slow, one-handed side stroke that, with the steady movement of her legs and feet, propelled her out into the stream.

Suddenly, the current grabbed her, whirled her around, and pulled her under. She came up sputtering. Struggling against the unsuspected strength of the current, she swam toward the opposite shore. At last, her feet touched bottom again, and she waded onto the rocks.

She reached for her bundle, and found it still hanging from her shoulder, but it was thoroughly soaked. She supposed the bread, at least, was no longer edible.

Hannah looked up. The cliff rose steeply in front of her. To climb it would be extremely difficult, if not impossible. She listened intently. She had heard no baying of hounds behind her for some time now. Maybe they had given up and gone home.

Suddenly, the deep bay of a bloodhound traveled over the water, joined by the baying of other hounds. They were closer than they had been the last time she had heard them. Blindly, she plunged back into the river and waded frantically upstream.

From *The Journey of Emilie...*

A scream—a man's scream—pierced the air. In the cabin doorway, a crowd leaned over a slumped figure. Feet pounding, Emilie and Frau Jurgen ran to see.

"Heinrich!"

"Saw . . ." groaned the injured man. "Slipped . . ."

"Cut the leg off his pants," ordered a terse voice.

Reaching the scene of the accident, Emilie gasped. Herr Schulz's left leg was gashed. A ribbon of blood seeped along the slit in his trousers, the loose threads soaking it up like millions of tiny wicks.

"Who's got a wad of tobacco?" hollered a man.

"Spider webs are what you want. A ball of them stuffed into a wound stops bleeding."

"*Ach*, where do we get spider webs off a brand-new cabin?"

"If Franz Borner weren't a temperance man, I'd have my little brown jug here to wash that out good."

Then Papa and Reinhard Jurgen jumped into the fray, Papa with prayer and Herr Jurgen with torn strips of shirt to wind around the cut. As Herr Schulz was helped into a wagon to be driven home, a quiet descended on the settlers.

"Praise God it didn't hit a blood vessel."

"Sliced to the bone, though."

"As long as infection doesn't set in . . ."

"He'll be off his feet awhile. He'll be needing help, that's for sure."

Abruptly, another neighbor moved to the doorway and took Herr Schulz's place.

"Should we call off the housewarming?" Emilie asked Frau

Zimmermann and Della Jurgen.

"Not at all," asserted Frau Zimmermann. "Look, the musicians are going to warm up already." Two men passed through the door, one with an instrument case and the other with a concertina. "Gottlieb Graf has his mouth organ too, just see if he doesn't. Accidents are a fact of life here." Frau Zimmermann shook her head. "We wish Heinrich well, but everything moves along. Come, girl, I'll help you lay your cabin's first fire. I have a special gift, too." The plump woman smiled.

Emilie entered the cabin. She felt a little thrill when Papa "closed" the door behind her by fitting it into its frame and beginning to hang it. The chatter and laughter of friends and neighbors warmed her, even before the firewood caught flame and heat radiated into the room.

"Now, the gift." Frau Zimmermann proudly handed Emilie a package, loosely wrapped in plain paper and tied with string. "Undo it carefully." Emilie eased the wrapping off to find a fold of feathers like the one Frau Zimmermann used to sweep her hearth.

"Your own turkey wing. A clean hearth is a clean room."

Emilie smiled, although something seemed to settle about her shoulders. She suspected "something" was named Responsibility. "Thank you, Frau Zimmermann."

The musicians started playing immediately, and neighbors began to dance, clap, and sing. "If we can still carry on like this after working so hard, I guess we're not so old after all," Frau Zimmermann remarked.

"Tough luck if we are," said Frau Graf, wife of the mouth-organ player. "Frontier life is not for the infirm."

"Rather than bemoan tough luck," chimed in another, "pray Heinrich Schulz is not among the infirm after today."

Troubled, Emilie stepped away from the group. She'd been ready to join the singing, to coax Heidi into a dance, but suddenly she was afraid. With one wrong slip of a tool, a strapping family man had become an invalid. However would she manage, keeping house alone in a new, wild country? How would her family cope if something happened to her?

"Emilie?" Frau Jurgen, holding Josef, spoke softly beside her. "Is it Herr Schulz you're thinking of?"

Emilie turned to her friend. "No," she said earnestly, "it's me." She drew a breath. "And it's strange to have a party without Mama and Karl here. Merrymaking on the ship was different. It wasn't actually our home."

Frau Jurgen nodded. "I know, Emilie. Erich's bed waits in our loft, and I don't know if that makes things easier or harder. With new homes built, we feel even more that we've gone on without our loved ones."

Emilie's gaze wandered to the built-in bed, its frame strung with a web of ropes holding the feather mattress. It was a double bed. Whether Mama's half would be empty for always, she couldn't bear to think. Was the future in Wisconsin really any surer than in Germany? It seemed shrouded in fog.

Frau Jurgen's hand crept onto Emilie's shoulder. "God doesn't reward our trust by leading us astray. Scripture gives us every right, and even a duty, to hope."

Emilie nodded. She needed to hope. "I'm going to find Heidi and ask if she'd like to dance."

Heidi, giggling, did take a few spins on the plank floor. Hilda Zimmermann danced shyly with a young man of about twenty. "They'll marry soon," another girl confided to Emilie. "Everyone knows it."

These moments of good cheer were short. Just as Emilie was about to dance a *schottische* with Heidi, Frau Zimmermann spoke a few innocent words that turned the party upside down.

"Emilie." She bustled over to the young people. "We've got bread, pickles, pretzels, cherries, and plates and forks for everything except the *kuchen*. Do you have plates we could use to serve the *kuchen?*"

Emilie understood in a flash that Mama would offer the

lusterware. What she didn't understand was why Heidi's shoulders stiffened under her hand. "Yes, Frau Zimmermann. I can unpack them easily."

Heidi fled.

"Heidi? I won't be long," Emilie called, but she knew Heidi wouldn't listen. She remembered how Heidi had played with the trunk latches on the ship and at the immigration station. Was she afraid of trunks, of their yawning mouths and dark insides, perhaps? Had she been assuring herself that the latches were fastened down tight?

"Your dishes seem to unnerve her somehow," Heidi's mother said, coming to help.

"Maybe it's good if I unpack them and store that trunk out of sight," Emilie agreed. They eased the trunk over the rough flooring, away from the dancing feet, and unsnapped the latches.

"I think the dessert plates are on the sides, on top of the dinner plates," Emilie said. She lifted newspaper and burlap from the top and picked up a cloth-wrapped plate. But something in the package shifted. One side of the cloth sagged too low. Emilie unwrapped the plate hurriedly.

"It's broken!" she cried, holding up two halves.

"This one, too." Frau Jurgen showed her a plate that appeared to have been bitten into.

Emilie sagged back on her heels. "No wonder they say not to bring china." She pulled plate after plate from the chest, pulled off the wrappings, then started on pieces from the middle so they wouldn't topple: sugar bowl, gravy boat, cups. Those that weren't shattered were at least badly chipped.

"Here, Frau Zimmermann can put *kuchen* on these." Emilie handed dishes to Hilda. "But we'll never use them again, will we? Unless we get desperately poor." Perhaps, she thought, they were desperately poor already.

"I'm sorry, Emilie," Frau Jurgen said gently. "I wonder if Heidi knew they had broken, and was worried we'd be angry?" She shook her head. "No, that makes no sense."

Emilie felt her eyes brimming.

"Emilie?"

"They're Karl's inheritance." Her throat worked. "Karl's inheritance is smashed."

"And one of his ties to the New World is smashed, too?" Frau Jurgen ventured.

Emilie's tears dribbled over.

Frau Jurgen wrenched the trunk aside and led Emilie out into the autumn dusk. "I don't want you to take this as a sign from God that Karl doesn't belong here."

"But what if he doesn't?" Emilie sobbed. "And if he doesn't come, Mama never will either."

"Oh, Emilie, I don't know. I can't pretend I do." Frau Jurgen put her arm around Emilie's shoulders and hugged tight. "I ask God to plant a desire in everyone's hearts to follow His way more than their own. I ask God to guide us through whatever comes."

Emilie sniffled. "Those are good things to pray."

"That part about following God's way more than our own? That's for us, too, not just Karl and Erich."

"It is?"

Frau Jurgen nodded. "Should God wish to leave them in Germany, it will be up to us to accept it. I remind myself often of His promise that all things work together for good when we love God and are called according to His purpose. Do you know that Scripture?"

"Romans 8:28. Papa reads it all the time now," Emilie said. "But I don't know if I understand it. Maybe I never did."

"God can see inside our hearts," Frau Jurgen said. "If we obey Him, and want to fulfill His purpose for us, He promises all things work out for good."

Emilie shivered in the chill air. "Like Meta coming over on Mama's ticket. But I don't see how Mama being left in Germany can be good."

"Maybe it isn't," said Frau Jurgen. "The verse says all things work together for good, not that each thing that happens is good in itself, or seems good right away."

Emilie pondered this.

"We might as well finish unpacking your dishes, and let your papa know what's happened if he doesn't already."

More cups and saucers came out of the chest, chipped and cracked. Emilie and Della Jurgen unwrapped every bundle as carefully as they would baby Josef, yet each one yielded disappointing shards of shiny copper and blue. People looked over their shoulders.

"Pity. You know what they say about bringing china."

"It's a shame, but dishes can be had in Sheboygan."

Emilie picked up the loose wrapping that she knew contained the cream pitcher. No hope for this piece. None at all.

She opened it—and gasped. Surprise made her let go, and it skidded down her lap.

"Oh!" Frau Jurgen caught the pitcher and lifted it. "Emilie! It's whole, and—" Whatever else she meant to say died on her lips.

The lusterware cream pitcher was stuffed with paper money.

DATE DUE
